Praise for *Stella*

"This tender novel from a dog's perspective will help readers understand the importance of animals in their lives. This empathetic read is also full of important themes and lessons for young readers—bravery, how to overcome fears, and that mistakes don't have to define us. A heartfelt dog story that readers young and old will enjoy."

—*School Library Journal*

"Endearing. Tender exploration of human-animal bonding. The book's suspenseful final third focuses on Cloe's interactions with bullies, forcing Stella to relive her own traumatic memories, and to act brave despite them. This is a circular but satisfying means for Stella to resolve her fears. Stella realizes that it is okay to have made mistakes in the past, and that love doesn't require working for approval . . . In the memorable novel *Stella*, a dog looks to heal—and find a home."

—*Foreword Reviews*

"A traumatized working dog has one last chance after the death of her handler. Stella, a bomb-sniffing beagle, has been in three foster homes since the death of her handler, Connie, in an explosion. Now she's got PTSD, and she panics at loud noises, fire, or being left alone. Unable to do anything for her, the humans plan to euthanize Stella until she receives a last-minute reprieve. An old friend of Connie's, a world-class dog trainer, decides to take on Stella's rehabilitation as a favor to her old friend. Through Stella's doggy point of view . . . readers are introduced to dog training with Esperanza and her 11-year-old daughter, Cloe. . . . As her bond with Cloe grows, Stella learns more about what Cloe's sometimes-strange smells mean when she first witnesses Cloe have an epileptic seizure. . . . Dog training, trauma recovery, and just enough urgency to keep it moving: a quiet pleasure."

—*Kirkus Reviews*

"The heartbeat of this pitch-perfect story about second chances and healing is a beagle named Stella. If you looked up the definition of loyalty and unconditional love, you'd see a picture of Stella. She'll win your heart!"

—Bobbie Pyron, award-winning author of *Stay*

"*Stella* is not only an emotionally intense adventure tale, but a special love story between dog and girl. So many lessons of love and courage, and the importance of animals to our mental—and physical—health. I adored it!"

—Sally J. Pla, award-winning author of
The Someday Birds

"Sweet, smart, and full of heart. Every reader will want their very own Stella!"

—Victoria J. Coe, author of
the Fenway and Hattie series

"Part Fenway and Hattie, part *The Poet's Dog,* readers will fall head over tails for Stella. A good dog, indeed."

—Kristin Gray, author of *The Amelia Six*

"A joyful celebration of the unbreakable bond between dogs and their humans, *Stella* is a heartfelt, tail-wagging treat. An enthusiastic paws-up for this middle-grade debut!"

—Melissa Roske, author of *Kat Greene Comes Clean*

Stella

McCall Hoyle

SHADOW
MOUNTAIN
PUBLISHING

For Connie—
mother-in-law, friend,
and caretaker of all the
beagles in heaven

First printed in hardback 2021
First printed in paperback 2022

This is a work of fiction. Characters and events in this book are products of the author's imagination or are represented fictitiously.

Library of Congress Cataloging-in-Publication Data

Names: Hoyle, McCall, author.

Title: Stella / McCall Hoyle.

Description: Salt Lake City : Shadow Mountain, [2021] | Includes references. | Audience: Ages 8–11. | Audience: Grades 4–6. | Summary: Stella used to be a bomb-sniffing dog, but after a terrible accident, she goes to live on a small family farm to recover from her fear of loud noises.

Identifiers: LCCN 2020035290 | ISBN 9781629729015 (hardback) | ISBN 978-1-63993-055-5 (paperback)

Subjects: LCSH: Dogs—Juvenile fiction. | CYAC: Dogs—Fiction. | Post-traumatic stress disorder—Fiction. | Human-animal relationships—Fiction. | Farm life—Fiction. | LCGFT: Fiction.

Classification: LCC PZ10.3.H837 St 2021 | DDC [Fic]—dc23

LC record available at https://lccn.loc.gov/2020035290

Printed in the United States of America   4/2022
PubLitho

10 9 8 7 6 5 4 3 2

You must do the thing
you think you cannot do.

—ELEANOR ROOSEVELT

Chapter One

My nose wakes up before the rest of me. A whole world of smells outside the open window of the house begs to be explored—wet grass, dead worms, and my absolute favorite: rabbits. My back leg quivers at the thought of chasing one of the brown balls of fluff. Pressing my nose against the thin metal bars of my crate, I inhale every detail of the morning.

My name is Stella.

I'm a beagle, and I was born to sniff.

And that's what I do.

Sniff. Sniff. And sniff.

The rabbits in the field out back smell almost as lovely as the cheese and crackers my new human left out on the counter all night. My nose twitches. It will rain today, and a skunk braved the back porch last night in search of food. There's so much to explore. It's impossible to be still.

My new human, Diana, sleeps until long after the sun has risen high, drying the sparkly dew from the grass. She breathes softly in the room down the hall, but my paws itch to be out on the trail with my old human.

A whimper catches in my throat when I think of Connie. She and I worked together at the airport. I used to love the airport and all the friendly people with all their interesting scents. Now, when I think about it, the hair on my back bristles. The last time Connie and I were there, bad, bad smells soaked the place. Chemical smells—chemicals that singed my eyes, burned my nose, and hurt Connie. A blaring ambulance took her far, far away. And she would never leave me if she could help it.

Thunder rumbles in the distance, but I tell myself to be still. Be good. Don't worry. It's just a storm. Connie said I was a good dog.

"Good girl, Stella. You're a good girl." That's what she said every day. Then she'd rub my ears or scratch me under the chin.

I miss her so much, it makes my stomach hurt sometimes, like when I was a pup and got into the trash and ate all the human food—the greasy chicken, the crumbled biscuits, and best of all, gravy! I whine when I think of Connie. Unable to stop myself, I jiggle the crate with my paw.

My new human, Diana, doesn't like whining, and she doesn't like gravy. Diana eats lots and lots of plants. And now, she's rolling over in the bed in the next room.

"Hush, Stella! It's too early," she scolds. Her smell paints every bit of the tiny house. When she kicks the sheets and blankets, she sends out a fresh wave of smells: the plants she made into juice before bed, and soap, and the unique tang of earth and light sweat that make her Diana, my new human.

Resting my head on my paws, I try to be quiet. But the wind picks up, and the room darkens despite the rising sun. My whiskers twitch and tingle, alert to the threat of lightning—alert to anything resembling an explosion, like the one at the airport. Lifting one ear, then the other, I listen for danger. My jaws click. Diana won't like it, but I lift my paw and rattle my crate again. I would be safer under the couch and less likely to howl, or dig, or get into trouble. Instead, I'm trapped in this useless crate.

At Connie's, I had a soft bed instead of a crate, with sheets that smelled like her.

"Stella, no!"

I move to the back of the cage, willing myself to be a good dog. But the pads of my paws moisten. Lightning flashes in the distance. I turn in tight circles, trying to calm myself. I miss the blankets in my bed at Connie's. I was brave with Connie, but even brave dogs need to burrow in cozy blanket nests when thunder shakes the house or when angry voices hang in the air.

The crate at Diana's has nothing but a slick foam pad on the bottom. I lie down on it for a few seconds but can't stay down. My paws need to move, to dig out a safe den under the porch or scratch out a cool spot under the bed. With nowhere to hide, my throat and sides tighten. My temperature rises. My mouth opens. Then the panting starts. I pause to give the gate another rattle.

Diana doesn't move. I circle three more times, but I can't control myself. Panic strikes. And when it strikes, it strikes. Instinct grips me, and I pant and dig. Pant and dig. My heart races. My paws work on their own. In no time, I've dug through the slippery foam down to the hard surface underneath.

The chilly floor of the crate cools the warm pads of my feet. I tear into a chunk of the pad with my teeth, shaking it back and forth vigorously. Lakes of white foam fall like snow onto the floor around the crate. As I dig, shred, and shake, the room brightens a little. The sun peeks through the clouds. The fist of fear gripping my chest relaxes. It seems the storm changed its mind, or the wind changed its direction. Sighing, I exhale and nose the hunks and shreds of foam into something resembling a nest, circle one more time, then curl up in the back of the crate and wait.

I ripped the pad, which wasn't good, but I was mostly

quiet and let my human sleep. I'm a good dog. Connie said so, and I could trust Connie. She was my best friend. Until the bad men with the bad-smelling chemicals at the airport took her away from me.

Lying very, very still in my nest of foam, I wait for Diana to release me. If she doesn't come soon, I will need to squat and relieve myself. And I know how humans feel about dogs squatting, and it's not good. Even Connie didn't like it when I was a pup and squatted on the carpet. Humans love their carpet and like to keep it clean.

The bed in the next room squeaks. My ears lift. The tip of my nose wiggles. Diana's scent cloud moves on the air. I smell her movement before her feet hit the floor, long before she rounds the corner to my spot in the hall.

I stand, wagging my tail. Maybe since she slept the best part of the day away—the early part where the smells are all fresh and held close to the ground by the moisture in the air—she might take me for a walk.

Her feet pad toward me. I stand hoping, hoping, hoping for a long walk or a big bowl of kibble. A little bite of bacon would be great too.

Then she turns the corner, and her eyes widen and her face scrunches in on itself.

"Bad dog!" She leans down to open the front of the crate, her face the color of a rubber ball. "Out," she shouts.

I hang my head. Connie never shouted, except for the

time when I was chasing a squirrel and ran in front of a truck on the road near our house. Her voice got really loud that day. But I don't understand why Diana is so upset. Ripping up a stiff, useless pad is not as bad as running in front of a big truck.

Diana likes to burrow in her blankets and pillows. Shouldn't I be allowed to burrow in mine? I wouldn't have dug in the pad and definitely wouldn't have ripped it to bits with my teeth if she hadn't locked me in the crate with a storm coming or left me alone for so long.

"Out!" she screams.

When I run past her, she nudges me with her foot. And, if you ask me, her nudge is a little too hard. I'm a tough beagle. That's what Connie said. But even tough beagles don't like rough feet on their behinds.

I race around the backyard, squatting several times to mark my territory and to make sure the raccoons and opossums that come around at night remember a dog lives here.

I'd like to track down the rabbits for a nice game of chase, but my insides ache with hunger, and I haven't forgotten the cheese and crackers on the counter. So I trot back to the house. But when I climb the three wooden steps to the back porch, something is terribly wrong. Diana must have forgotten I was outside because the door is closed tight.

I glance from one end of the porch to the other. Maybe

I'm supposed to eat my morning meal outside today. But there's no bowl, no kibble, and even stranger, Diana has moved my crate out here.

I may not understand everything about humans, but I know enough to know that I've got a big problem. My crate *should not* be stuck out here on the porch, and neither should I.

Chapter Two

I whine for hours, but the back door remains shut. For the next couple of days, there's almost no sign of Diana except for a few words here and there when she nudges a bowl of kibble outside for me. I try to whimper and show her how sorry I am, but she comes and goes so quickly it's hard to make her understand.

On the third day, I cannot take it any longer. I start to dig. And dig. And dig. But the cool earth between the pads of my paws does little to reduce the tightness in my chest. That's when I start to bark and bay. It's also when the neighbor opens his door to shout at me and kick the trash can on his porch. I jump every time the metal can rattles, then I slink to the far side of the yard in search of a place to hide.

After what seems like a lifetime, Diana comes to her

senses. "Okay, girl," she says, "we're going to have to try something different." She bends down, giving my head a little pat. When her fingers brush my ears, my toenails *click-clack* on the wooden boards. I bounce around her feet as she opens the door to let me in. My tail thumps her legs, the walls, and several pieces of furniture as she drags my crate back to its place in the hall.

"Let's try this again." She squats down and replaces the shredded foam pad with a soft blanket then takes me for a long walk in the woods.

Later that day, a nice man comes to eat pizza with Diana, and my tail thumps even harder. He is a very smart man who knows how to quietly drop bits of cheesy crust under the table without Diana noticing. After they scrape their plates, they head into the room with the big TV.

I'm not allowed on the couch, but that's okay. My belly is full. I'm sleepy from walking in the woods all morning, and I'm very, very thankful to be back inside where I belong. I curl up at the man's feet. They talk to each other then watch other people talk to each other on the big TV.

"She seems like a sweet dog." The man rubs me gently with his socked foot.

"Oh, she is. I think she would be a great dog if someone could stay home with her all the time. But she goes crazy if you leave her alone. And even if I am home, a thunderstorm or a car backfiring or any loud noise drives her totally berserk."

"Whatever happened to her must have been terrible," he says. He sounds sad, which is confusing. How can he be sad when he's rubbing my belly and making me feel so good?

Humans can be that way though—confusing. Even the smartest dog in the world couldn't learn all of their words. They use so many of them and lots of times the sound of the words doesn't match the smell of the person's feelings. They can use really calm words even when their hearts are racing and they smell nervous. But they also rub bellies, and give kisses, and go for long walks. So they're worth it. If you ask me, they would all be a lot better off with a good dog to help them manage all the up-and-down emotions they feel every day.

Stretching out on my side, I sigh and close my eyes. The man's soft sock rubs the hard-to-reach spot under my front leg. My eyes grow heavy.

"She seems pretty relaxed right now." He laughs, and I melt a little deeper into the carpet.

"The lady at the canine facility said she was injured in an explosion at the airport." Diana's voice is softer than usual.

"I remember seeing that on the news. What happened to the dog's handler was awful." The nice man gets down on the floor with me and rubs my belly with his warm hand. He lifts one of my long ears and rubs tiny circles near the edge, and I dissolve like snow flurries.

Finally, finally, I'm getting somewhere with these humans. Now if I could just get myself together and be a really good dog all of the time and not go *berserk*, Diana and I might be able to get along, and maybe I could even figure out a way to find Connie.

"I would take her if I could." He keeps talking, but he doesn't forget to keep rubbing. Smart man.

Diana joins us on the floor. "You'd get kicked out of your apartment. She needs to be out in the country with a family and children. They warned me at the canine facility, but I thought I could make it work with the big yard and all."

Diana's hand joins the man's on my body. She gently pats my side. Between the man's ear massage and her patting, I feel almost like a pup again, like when I was wedged in the nest with my mother. She would take turns licking my face and then my sisters' and brothers' faces. I loved it when we slept, and I got the spot near her chest and could feel her heart thumping against my fur.

"She needs to be with someone who doesn't work—someone who's home during the day. She's better, even with the loud noises, if she's not alone."

"What will they do with her?"

"I don't know. I'm her third foster home, and I can't

afford to keep her. When she panics, she destroys the house. I tried moving her out to the yard, but she digs. And one of the neighbors complained last week about all the barking."

They get very quiet. Diana's hand goes still. I snuffle to remind them to keep petting. We stay like this late into the evening until the man leaves. Then Diana takes me out to do my business. When we come back in, she kisses me and tells me I'm a good dog. But she sounds really sad.

Thankfully, she doesn't put me in my crate. She lets me sleep on the floor beside her bed. In the morning, she gets up before the dew has dried, takes me for a walk, and feeds me my morning meal.

And there is bacon.

Bacon!

She sprinkled tiny bits of bacon on top of my meal.

"You want to go for a ride?" she asks as I lick the bowl one last time, savoring the smoky, meaty taste.

Ride? I know that word. It's one of my all-time favorite words. Do I want to go for a ride? That's like asking if I want to chase the fluffy, brown rabbits out back that zig and zag. Yes! Of course, I want to go for a ride.

A minute later, she fastens a silly jeweled collar around my neck. Diana can't help it. She doesn't know I'm a working dog and supposed to wear a serious black collar and harness. She leaves the crate in the house, and when we get outside to her car, she lets me jump on the front seat. I can hardly believe it. She must have forgiven me for ripping up the useless pad, and squatting in the house, and digging holes in the backyard.

"You really are a good girl," she says as we drive away. She sounds sad, so I nudge her hand until it rests on my side. Most humans like to lay their hands on a dog's side. It makes their heart rate slow down, and they seem to relax.

"I'm sorry I can't keep you." She still sounds sad, but she's petting me, so I figure we're all good. After driving for a very long time, the smell of dirt and trees is replaced by more and more exhaust from cars and trucks. The harsh smells of hot asphalt and cold steel prick my nose. I think we're nearing the city—my and Connie's city.

I stand up to look out the window. It's definitely my city. I see the train that runs on tracks above the ground and around tall buildings. I can't be certain, but I think we might be going to see Connie. I'm so busy looking out the window, I don't hear the airplane until it's right overhead. Then my head jerks, and my nose smacks the window. I whine. I want to see Connie, but I don't want to go to the airport ever, ever again. I sit down on the seat for a second, trying to figure out what's happening.

"It's okay, girl. I'm taking you home." She rests her hand on my back.

Home? I know that word, and I want to go home. But

home is with Connie. Or is it with Diana? Or is it with the old man I had for a few weeks before Diana?

I step on the door handle to be taller and peer out the window better. Diana opens it a crack, and I smell the dog park and the place with hundreds and hundreds of children. And then I see the big white building and smell lots and lots of dogs and know we are going back to the canine facility—back to Connie.

I can hardly believe it. I'm glad Diana and I worked out our differences, and I hope she will find a very good dog of her own. But I belong with Connie. For the first time in a long while, I'm so focused on something good, I forget to worry about all the bad things in the world like airplanes roaring overhead or trucks rumbling on busy roads. I'm going back to my person.

To Connie.

I'm so excited. I force myself to sit tall and still on the front seat, but my mouth opens a little. I let my tongue hang out as I think about my best friend.

Connie.

Connie.

Connie.

Chapter Three

As we approach the door, I smell lots of dogs—old dogs like Rocky and new dogs I don't recognize. These dogs won't know what to think about Diana's sparkly collar, but who cares? I'm about to see Connie, Connie, Connie.

Diana pulls the glass door open, and I smell familiar humans. The strongest scents belong to Ava, who sits at the front desk and moves papers around all day, and Jake, who is the top man and drinks lots and lots of the hot brown liquid with the strong, biting smell.

Underneath it all, there might be a hint of Connie, but I can't be certain.

Ava looks up from her papers when the bells on the door jingle then trots over to me. "Oh, sweet Stella. You're back. We've missed you, sweet girl." She rubs my ears, wiggling my head back and forth gently, then leans in for a kiss. And she smells delicious, like donuts, milk, and kindness. But she sounds sad too, and I wonder what's wrong with everyone today.

It's a very, very happy day.

Ava stands up like she's tired and extends her hand to Diana.

"I'm so sorry—" Diana stops in the middle of her words.

Ava shakes her head. The sad water forms at her eyes, and the smell of salt mixes with all her sugary goodness.

"I tried. I really did." Diana looks down at me.

"I know." Ava rests a hand on Diana's arm. "We were worried she might not make it. Sometimes dogs don't recover from that kind of trauma—"

There are too many starts and stops in their words. This isn't normally how the human talking works. When a door behind Ava's desk swings open, I jump. But it's just Jake. He hasn't changed since the last time I saw him. He stands very tall and commands respect, like the top dog in a pack. And he smells exactly the same—all dark beans soaked in water, mixed with steak, and chicken, and ham.

I wag my tail, but wait for him to call me before crossing the room to greet him.

He lowers himself to the floor. "Hi, Stella. Why are you back, girl? We wanted you to make a new life for yourself."

He looks up at Diana. But Diana just shakes her head again as the salty water drips on her cheeks. Jake goes to her and places a big hand on her shoulder. "You tried. We all tried. It just wasn't meant to be. Some dogs never get over that type of violent explosion. Sometimes they can't recover from losing their handlers, and Stella suffered both at the same time. We'll take care of her."

I wag my tail. We should all be happy.

Diana leans down to rub the loose skin on my neck. She kisses the top of my head. I understand that she's sad, so I lick her face. She smiles, and a sobbing breath she must have been holding back shoots out of her mouth.

Jake takes her gently by the arm and leads her to the door where they speak in quiet voices. She smiles at me one more time then hurries out the door, the salty water still streaming down her cheeks.

If I could, I would lick her face and nudge her hand and sit with her, but I know my true place is with Connie. There are lots and lots of dogs in the world, and Diana will find her dog. Or her dog will find her. That's how it works. I belong with Connie.

"Come on, girl," Jake says. "Let's go see Doc Collins."

Oh, I know that name—Doc Collins. It belongs to the man with gentle hands and the gentle voice. He smells like medicine but gives lots of treats. I like Doc Collins a lot, but I'm here to see Connie.

When we pass through the door behind Ava's desk, I hear dogs barking back in the kennels. Near the end of the hall, I smell a whiff of Connie, coming from the room where she used to move papers. But something is wrong. Connie's smell is old. She hasn't been here in a long time.

I glance up at Jake. Just then, Doc Collins steps into the hall in the funny coat he wears that brushes the big part of his legs.

"Oh, Stella girl," he says.

Enough with the *Oh, Stella girl*. Don't they know I'm here to see Connie?

And why does Doc Collins smell sad and anxious? He's never anything but calm and cool.

"Put her in my examining room, Jake. I need to weigh her and find a syringe."

"Okay, Doc." Jake bends down to pick me up and cuddle me to his side. He never handles dogs like babies. Jake is serious and focused on work. Always.

Which means . . . something is terribly wrong.

Doc glances at the collar-like strap on his wrist. "Just let me finish with Esperanza, and I'll be right back."

Jake takes me to another room slathered in dog and medicine smells. I expect him to place me on the cold, slippery table. That's what happens when humans bring dogs into these rooms. Instead, he sits with me in his lap, rubs me behind the ears, and speaks lots and lots of soft, slow words.

"It's not your fault, Stella. You're a good girl. You deserve better. Nobody wants you to suffer." He rubs his face against my neck. "Doc's been doing this a long time. He says the kindest thing to do is put you out of your misery—that you'll never be the same without valuable work and a competent handler."

I understand the *good girl* part, but I don't believe it. If I were a *good girl*, Connie would be here to take me home. If I were a *good girl*, I would have directed Connie to the bad chemicals faster. I wouldn't have been confused by the air blowing in through the open doors.

And then Jake and Doc Collins wouldn't have to *put me out of my misery*. I know what that means too. I was in the hall when they put Sarge *out of his misery* after the accident in the snow last winter. It means they put you into a deep, deep sleep, and your dog smell changes. You're just the outside of a dog, and you don't wake up. Ever.

They put you in a box.

If they *put me out of my misery*, I'll never see Connie again.

I whimper like a pup. Jake rubs his face against my cheek. I lick his hand, hoping he'll change his mind and give me another chance. I will not dig holes, or tear pads, or squat on the carpet. I won't chase rabbits. I'll even work at the airport if Jake will give me one more chance to be a good dog and find Connie.

Chapter Four

While we wait for Doc Collins, I continue to lick Jake's hand. I don't want him to be sad. None of this is his fault. His chest is wide and warm, and he's a great ear and chin scratcher. Surely, he won't let anyone put me to sleep or seal me in a box.

As his hand makes its way down the back of my neck, the door swings open. It's Doc Collins, and there's a tall woman with dark hair and dark eyes, standing behind him. She commands respect like Jake. Even from across the room, I smell dogs on both of them. But the woman also smells like flowers—fancy flowers—the kind humans buy in stores, not the kind that grow in rabbit fields or forests. There are also hints of grass, dirt, animals I don't recognize, and a child.

"Jake, this is Esperanza." Doc Collins gestures back and forth between the two humans.

She steps forward to do the handshake greeting that humans enjoy and then smiles down at me.

"Hi, Stella Bella," Esperanza says, smiling and tugging gently on my ear.

Finally, someone is in a good mood.

"Esperanza's here to test some of the new pups for us and help us decide which ones to place in the explosive detection program and which ones to keep for the tracking program. And she's interested in Stella." Doc ruffles the fur on top of my head.

"Stella? You know she can't work anymore. You retired her." Jake squeezes me tighter against his chest.

"Esperanza thinks she might be able to rehabilitate her and find her a home."

Jake shakes his head. His heart rate and breathing speed up a notch. "We've tried that. Three times. It's not fair to keep bouncing her from one place to another. At some point, we have to admit enough is enough."

"Esperanza is a world-renowned dog trainer." Doc nods to the strong woman.

She smiles and lifts her shoulders. "I've been training dogs since I was twelve. It's my life. Most recently, I've been focusing on sheep-herding trials and working dogs."

I open my mouth to match Esperanza's toothy smile and give my tail a weak thump.

"Doc—" Jake doesn't seem as excited about the nice woman as Doc does.

"I know we said three times. But Esperanza was Connie's friend. She's one of the best dog trainers in the world. She's willing to take Stella on for free. She wants to do this for Connie. And I think we should give her a chance."

They're talking about my Connie. Maybe I misunderstood them earlier. Maybe Connie is somewhere else, and they're going to take me to her after Doc and Jake finish talking to me and petting me.

I lick Jake's face as Esperanza holds her arms out to him. He doesn't move. After a long pause, he kisses the top of my head and hands me to her. She holds me against her chest, using one hand between my front legs to keep me steady and using the other hand to tug gently on the scruff of my neck, which reminds me of my mother and of being a puppy. My body goes limp like a wet blanket across her arm. She has nice breathing and a calm heartbeat.

"I'll take good care of her. I promise." She smiles at Jake then at Doc Collins. "Connie would want me to work with her. I'm confident I can help her, but if can't, I won't bring her back. I promise. I'll take her to my vet, so no matter what, you don't have to worry about her anymore."

Doc Collins pats Jake on the back. "Trust me. I think Esperanza is an answer to our prayers."

"Okay, Doc. I'm trusting you on this one." He gestures with his hand for us to head back into the hallway.

When we pass Ava on the way out, she breaks off a piece of her sandwich and offers it to me. I gobble it down before anyone decides I shouldn't have human food then lift my nose to sniff for Connie. All I smell is the faded, old scent that I smelled when Diana and I first arrived.

Doc and Jake walk us to Esperanza's car, which is more than a car but not exactly a truck. It has a big door on the side that slides open and dog crates stacked one on top of the other inside. I've never seen or smelled anything like it. Esperanza places me in a top crate beside a long window on the side opposite the door. She slides the door shut then goes around to the front and climbs into the seat behind the big wheel, and we're off.

The fancy flower smell drifts from a large circle of flowers propped against the front seat. The overpowering scent doesn't seem to bother Esperanza. She keeps the windows rolled up tight.

I don't know whether to be thankful that we're leaving and I didn't get *put out of my misery* or worried that Connie's place and her people are drifting farther and farther away. I'm not any closer to finding her now than I was this morning.

My stomach gurgles as the distance between us and the canine facility expands. After some time, fewer and fewer cars and trucks pass by my window. The tall buildings are replaced by tall trees. When the urge to do my business hits, I stand up in the crate. Esperanza is a smart dog lady. She seems to understand my urgent need.

"Relax, Stella Bella. We're almost there. We're going to say goodbye to Connie."

I don't like the way she says *Connie* and *goodbye* in the same group of words.

She pulls into an interesting park. There are no children or other dogs. There is none of the equipment children climb and swing on. But there are rows and rows of rectangular, flat stones sticking up out of the ground in straight lines.

I nudge the front of the crate with my nose. I really, really need to squat.

"Okay, girl, let's go find Connie," Esperanza says.

Wagging my tail, I wait as she parks the vehicle in the shade under a long row of trees then comes around to open the big sliding door and clip a leash to my collar. When I hop to the ground, she gives me time to sniff the tires and mark several nearby trees. After a few minutes of sniffing, she tugs lightly on my collar, and we head back to the vehicle. She holds my leash in one hand and hangs the strong-smelling circle of flowers in the crook of her other arm.

We proceed to weave back and forth through the stones

that stick out of the ground. The place is alive with bird chatter and the scent of squirrels and field mice and rabbits. Beneath all the alive smells is the smell of decaying wood buried underground and the smell of the outside of human bodies.

I know this smell. I recognize it from the day Doc Collins put Sarge into the deep, deep sleep and then placed him in the box. And I remember it from a night in the city with Connie when she gave me the command to *find*, and I found the burning chemical smell on the body of a man lying in a ditch on the side of the road.

Confused, I lift my head and stand very still. It's a Connie smell. I lower my head to the ground. Exhaling through my nose, I stir up scents from the grass. My long, thick ears trap the smells, concentrate them, and send them back down to my nose.

It's definitely Connie.

But it's not my Connie.

It's the still-sleeping-shell-of-Connie smell.

I whimper but press forward in case I'm confused by the light wind and the distracting smells of decaying wood, silent sleeping humans, and all the little creatures that call this park home.

Tugging at the leash, I pull Esperanza to a small stone standing near the back of the park. Keeping my head and ears lifted, I sit on high alert on the ground above where

Connie is sleeping. My tail stiffens, and I can't help it, I whine.

"Yes, Stella. Good girl. You found her." She slides the circle of flowers off her arm and props them against the standing stone. Then she sits beside me on the grass. "Now, it's time for you to move on, girl. She's not coming back."

Panting, I scratch at Esperanza's hand with my paw, trying to tell her to do something—to find. Find Connie. But she just sits there with her arm draped across my back. The sun drops lower in the sky. It won't be long until it drops behind the tall trees. But I'll sit here all night if there's any chance Connie will come back.

"Come on, Stella Bella. She's not coming back. Let's get you home and get you better." She touches her fingers to her lips then presses her fingers to the stone. "Goodbye, Connie."

I whimper as she tugs on the leash and guides me back to the big vehicle with all the crates. I don't squirm or whine when she closes the gate on the front. Connie is gone. I made a mistake that day at the airport, and she's gone.

She's not coming back.

And I don't care how much this smart dog lady tries to help or what kind words she says to me.

I'm a bad dog. And that's never going to change.

Chapter Five

This has been the longest car ride of my life. The flat city fell away ages ago. Now, the vehicle climbs up the biggest hills I've ever seen—so big and so rocky, the setting sun is hidden behind their peaks. The steep incline causes me to slide to the back of the crate. I try scrambling up toward the front for a better view several times, but each time my toenails slip on the hard, slick plastic underneath me. Eventually, I give up, curl into a ball, and hunker down, waiting to see how this journey will end.

"We're home, Stella Bella," Esperanza says when we finally turn off the smooth, hilly road and travel down a lane bumpy with rocks.

I lift my nose and flare my nostrils at the word *home*. This is not my home. But it seems to be the end of our journey. She stops her vehicle in front of a large wooden building. Before she slides the door open, I smell many strange plants and animals. There is a whole flock of creatures that smell vaguely like Connie's old sweaters and make a horrible bleating racket.

Esperanza opens her door and steps down to the rocky driveway. I'm inhaling the details of this strange new world when she slides the big door on the side of the vehicle open. Standing, I twitch my nose side to side as she opens the front of the crate and clips a leash to my collar.

"Come on, girl," she says, her voice kind but firm.

I want to stay in the crate, but I have no choice. She's the top human, so I hop down to the gravelly drive. Scents tug my head one way then the other. My eyes follow, drinking in the new surroundings. There's enough lush grass for an entire city of dog parks, or rabbit fields, or whatever the strange white creatures grazing in the fields are. An enormous white dog stands proudly over the funny creatures dotting the field. He glances in our direction but doesn't wag his tail. I've seen working dogs like him before, the kind who think they're too good to be with humans or even other dogs.

I'm not here to make friends, so I don't wag my tail either.

"Mama. Mama."

I jump when a girl shouts from the porch of a small house tucked in the shade of several towering trees.

"Hey, sweet girl!" Esperanza says, opening her arms for the running child.

"A beagle! What's its name?" the girl asks when she untangles herself from her mother's arms.

"Cloe, this is Stella. Stella, meet Cloe."

"She's adorable," Cloe says, bending down and offering me her hand.

Instead of towering over me like so many humans do when they greet a dog, she lowers herself so she's level with my eyes and nose. And she extends her hand, palm up for me to sniff, which is way better than having a strange human touch the top of your head before you've had a chance to get to know them.

The scent swirling from her cupped little hand might be the loveliest smell of any human I've ever smelled. She eats cookies—that's for sure—and spends time in the green grass that carpets every inch of space around the house and the big brown animal building. And she smells like cardboard and paper. I know that smell—it's books.

Books are good. I know a thing or two about them. One, don't eat them. That's as bad as squatting on the carpet. Two, very kind humans like to sit quietly with them for long periods of time. Connie certainly did anyway. She would study the pages inside, her eyes scanning back and forth, back and forth, as she spoke soothing words aloud to me.

Her favorite book was large with a very old, very

wise-looking woman on the front. Connie would repeat certain words over and over again as she looked at the big book. Her favorite group of words was *you must do the thing you think you cannot do.* She would repeat those words—*you must do the thing you think you cannot do*—over and over, like they were really important.

If I planned to make friends with Cloe, I think I would like it very much if she spoke soothing words to me from her favorite books. But I'm not here to make friends, and I'm distracted by another smell. Underneath the yummy cookie-grass-book smell is something else—a faint sour smell.

It reminds me of the vinegar-water solution the trainers at the canine facility used to clean the boxes and toys they used to train us. But it's not that smell exactly. There's also a hint of metal to it. And the smell isn't on Cloe's skin or clothes. The smell is part of her.

"Why don't you take her for a walk while I water the other animals," Esperanza says, handing my leash to Cloe and kissing the top of her head.

"Sure," Cloe says, leading me away from the vehicle. We head up a rocky hill that curves around the big building to an enormous flat area filled with obstacles, sort of like the ones we trained with at the canine facility, except these are bright and colorful like children's equipment on a play-ground. She leads me to a man-made tunnel.

"Want to try the tunnel, Stella?" She points her small hand at the entrance to the tunnel.

I glance inside. It's dark and damp in there. I'd try it—if Connie were here and commanded it. But this isn't a command, and I have no plans to torture myself. Ignoring the tunnel, I glance off into the distance. I don't want to be here. I really don't want to be anywhere without Connie.

But if I have to be here, at least I ended up with wise dog people. The girl seems to understand my body language, and we head off across the sandy field, leaving the dark tunnel behind. We're making progress toward a nice patch of grass lined with trees when she pauses at an unfamiliar piece of equipment. One end of the structure touches the ground. The other points up to the sky.

I sniff the end touching the ground. It smells like dogs—lots of healthy, athletic dogs.

"It's a teeter-totter, Stella," she says. Cloe reaches for the end that is pointing to the sky and pulls down. When she does, the board falls to the ground with a menacing thump.

I leap straight into the air. The sudden noise sounds like a muffled explosion, and the vibration of the ground shakes my paws. In an instant, I'm back in the airport. People are screaming. Smoke and dust and debris float in the air, and I can't see or smell Connie. I've lost her. Again.

Lowering my head, I whine. My back legs tremble,

shaking my entire body. My heart thumps so hard, it hurts. I worry it might burst out of my chest. I want to run—to escape—but the short leash won't allow it.

I whine again, and Cloe plops down in the sand beside me, pulling me into her lap and against her chest. After some time, my stiff body relaxes a little.

"I'm sorry, girl. It's okay. I won't let anything hurt you." Her steady heart beats softly against my side.

Thankfully, she doesn't try to make me smell or investigate the horrifying equipment. That had been Diana's way of dealing with things that scared me. We had to confront everything that alarmed me again and again. When she learned I was afraid of thunder, she quit playing songs on her music box and started playing loud storm sounds over and over. When she realized I chewed furniture and dug in the carpet when left alone, she left me in my crate for longer and longer periods of time. I always got the sense that she was trying to help me, but it only made things worse.

This girl, who I've barely met, seems to understand what I need more than the last three adults who have cared for me.

"You're okay, girl. I've got you," Cloe repeats over and over as she holds me firmly to her chest.

We sit like that for a long time, and eventually my heart stops hurting. When she rubs her forehead against my neck, waves of dark hair tickle my whiskers. I squirm and lick her face. The sound of her laugh is nice—all light and tinkly.

Eventually, we head over to the soft grass. Cloe doesn't rush me as I search for the perfect spot to do my business. When I'm finished, we retrace our steps across the flat sandy area with the play equipment. I pull to the end of the leash to give the teeter-totter plenty of space.

"Mom!" Cloe calls as we descend the gravelly hill.

"In the barn," Esperanza grunts from a big building with a dirt floor.

As we approach, she cuts open large cloth bags. The contents inside give off a wave of corn and molasses. A dog watches her. His head rests on his front legs, but he's alert. I recognize his scent. His smell was on Esperanza when we first met back at the canine facility. He stands, moving toward me with purpose, his tail low and relaxed.

Cloe drops the leash, allowing me to greet him on equal terms. There is nothing more embarrassing or uncomfortable for a dog than meeting a strange off-leash dog for the first time while she's unable to move about naturally.

He smells all right. He's not too pushy. Not too old. Not too young. And definitely in good health. We stand head to tail for a minute checking each other out. It doesn't take long for him to turn back to Esperanza though. He's obviously more interested in her than he is in me, or anything else for that matter. She's his human, and he's her dog. That's as plain as the nose on my face.

Esperanza beams down at us. "Good boy, Nando. Stella, this is Fernando. We call him Nando. Nando, meet Stella."

He glances at me then turns back to meet her eyes. He's really intense—thin and fit. I bet he can run fast and for a long time. He might even be able to catch the rabbits that always outrun me. His size and shape are average as far as dogs go. But he has penetrating eyes and isn't afraid to maintain eye contact with Esperanza for long periods of time. And his eyes are paler than any dog's I've ever seen.

"I'm about finished here," Esperanza says. "Why don't you put Stella in the empty crate in the feed room?"

Cloe's head whips around. "She can't sleep out here alone, Mama. She's scared."

"That's precisely the reason she needs to sleep out here. She needs the company of other animals." Esperanza's words sound like a command, even though she doesn't say it like Connie would.

"I tried to show her how the teeter-totter works, and she nearly jumped out of her skin. I've never seen a dog so scared." Cloe sits down on an overturned bucket and scratches me behind the ears.

"Stella was in an explosion at the airport. Her handler died. She has what's called post-traumatic stress disorder— sort of like the dachshund we worked with last winter, but much worse. Loud noises, thunder, being left alone—almost anything can cause her to panic."

Esperanza turns over another bucket, sits down beside Cloe, and places a hand on the girl's knee. "It's very serious, Cloe. We may not be able to help her."

"We'll help her." The girl nods. Her dark eyes thoughtful, she runs her small hand from the top of my head, all the way down my back, to the tip of my tail. When she does, my tail thumps the floor.

Esperanza lifts her hand from the girl's knee, places it under her chin, and tilts her face, so they're eye to eye. "When she panics, she can't help it. She shakes, barks, digs, drools. It's like she thinks she's going to be attacked. She thinks she's in serious danger and will do anything to escape the situation. She might even hurt herself trying to escape from whatever it is she thinks is dangerous. As a dog trainer, it's my responsibility to either help her or do what's most humane."

I glance back and forth between the two of them. They're talking about me—that's for sure—but using so many words. It's hard to understand much beyond my name and the word *crate*.

Cloe looks really sad, so I nuzzle my head underneath her hand, trying to take away her sadness.

"Can she sleep in my room just for one night?" Cloe turns her sad eyes to her mother.

"Absolutely not."

"She'll be scared out here."

"Cloe, she's a dog—a sweet dog—but still a dog. I think she'll actually be more comfortable out here with Nando and some of the other animals. I don't think it will do for either of us to get too attached to her until we see how things are going to work out."

"Mama, please, just one night."

"You don't need an anxious dog interrupting your sleep. Maybe after we get to know her better." Esperanza speaks in the firm voice of a top human and turns back to her bags of sweet-smelling corn.

Cloe stands up, but her shoulders sag. Grabbing the leash from the ground, she pulls on my collar. "Okay. Come on, Stella. I guess you'll be okay out here with Nando. I'll check on you first thing in the morning. I promise."

I follow, glancing up at her and wagging my tail. We walk down the center of the barn. Large rooms, sort of like crates, hold large animals that make rustling sounds as they munch on very dry, very old-smelling grass. I put a little bounce in my step, hoping Cloe will smile and the sadness will leave her.

I'm so focused on her that I don't see or smell the fat orange cat blocking the center aisle until I almost step on him. He closes his eyes and pretends not to care, but the tip of his tail lifts then pats the floor. I know what that means.

Diana's neighbor had a cat, who I tried to make friends with when I was alone in the backyard. But every time I got within playing distance, the cat closed its eyes and smacked the tip of its tail to the ground. If I came any closer, it hissed. One time it even caught my nose with its nails. Those nails were much smaller than mine but also much sharper.

"Stella, this is Oscar," Cloe says. "He's kind of a loner, but he's a good cat."

As we pass Oscar, I hug her lower leg, keeping a safe distance from his nails. The cat's eyes follow us into a room stacked with huge tubs and more buckets. The world's largest dog crate sits in the corner. My ears and tail sag. The bounce in my step dies. I know where this is going.

"Kennel up," Cloe says in a cheerful voice. But I don't feel too cheerful. When she points at the enormous crate, I slink inside.

"Good girl, Stella," she says. "Good girl."

I wag my tail, hoping she'll change her mind. At least the crate is lined with soft towels that smell like her and Esperanza. And I'm really tired. So when Cloe turns her back, I scratch the towels a few times, circle twice, and plop down with a long sigh. As she leaves the room, she flicks a switch on the wall, and the room goes dark.

"Good night, Stella," she says. "I'll see you first thing in the morning."

Lifting one ear and then the other, I listen to the sound of her receding footsteps. Then I'm alone. And I don't do *alone* very well. Beagles need a pack. For most of my life, I had Connie—the best pack of all.

Of course, she left me alone at times. But I always knew she was coming back—until the day at the airport when she didn't come back. Now I know she will never be coming back, and it scares me—really scares me—even though I tell myself there's nothing to be scared of. And I can't control myself. I do bad things when humans leave me alone— things that make them angry—like digging and scraping my nose on the floor, and howling, and panting, and drooling.

I really, really don't want to be alone tonight, but I don't want to be a bad dog either. And I don't want to disappoint this girl, Cloe.

Thankfully, Nando comes to lie in the doorway to the room full of buckets, so I'm not completely alone. At least, I have another dog with me—a dog who closes his eyes and falls asleep almost as soon as he stretches out on the wood floor.

Despite Nando's company and the soft blankets, my mouth starts to water.

My back legs tremble.

I have a bad feeling that Nando and I are in for a very long night.

Chapter Six

Somehow, I survive this night and the next several nights, but it isn't easy being out here without any humans. Nando is a very brave dog. He never leaves the feed room during the night. When a tree limb falls with a horrible clatter on the barn roof late one night, I jump so high I bang my head on the ceiling of my crate. Then I try to dig my way out, even though I know good and well these crates are escape proof. My nose burns from the repeated scraping against the crate floor.

Instead of getting annoyed and leaving though, Nando moves closer to my crate—the closest he's ever slept. Each time I start to pant or scrape or dig, he stands, gives me a quick, firm bark in the face, then returns to his spot on the floor. I get the gist of what he means—*Stop. Go to sleep.*

It's hard though. I wake every few minutes but

somehow make it through the night without bloodying my nose or paws or shredding the soft blankets lining the crate.

Nando and I are very different. I don't know that we'll ever be best friends, but I'm certainly learning to respect him. In addition to watching over me at night, he has a very important farm job. He sticks to Esperanza like he's tied to her lower leg with an invisible leash. Twice a day, the two of them go out into the field with the white creatures. I've learned the name for them—sheep. I'm learning all sorts of other new farm-and-barn words as well.

While they're out in the field, Esperanza shouts commands to Nando and whistles. I don't understand the words but I know they're commands because Nando chases the sheep in different patterns based on what Esperanza shouts or how she whistles, and her whistles are impressive.

I learned the big white dog I saw on the first evening is named Gus. He's a loner, like Oscar. In fact, I've never seen him leave the field to enter the house or the barn. He even takes his meals with the flock in the field. When Esperanza and Nando move the sheep, he holds back and watches. As soon as they finish their work, he moves in close again to watch over the flock. That seems to be his job—staring at the sheep, all day and all night—and he seems to think it makes him very important.

I don't have a job. I have a routine—wake up with the rooster when the sun rises, wait for Esperanza or Cloe, and eat my morning meal. Depending on the weather, I either go for a walk with Esperanza or Cloe or sniff around the fenced pasture at the front of the farm. Then I hang out in the barn until my evening meal.

Today Cloe and Esperanza enter the barn together. "Good morning, Stella," they say at the same time. I'm on my feet in an instant with my mouth pulled back in a smile. Nando barks excitedly at them, and they laugh.

"Good morning, handsome," Esperanza says and ruffles the fur on the top of his head.

My tail wags so hard at their closeness and at the smell of the eggs and beans they ate for breakfast that it rattles the crate.

"You want to eat, girl?" Cloe slides the lock on the gate, freeing me to bound around her feet as Esperanza pours dog food into two bowls on the counter. At the tinkling sound of kibble on metal, my mouth waters. I plop my be-hind on the floor and sit perfectly still, like a very good dog.

Yes, yes, yes! I want to eat. Before my bowl hits the floor, I'm inhaling the food. After three good licks to make sure I didn't miss a crumb, I trot out into the barn to take care of the second most important task of the day—doing my business.

"Wait for me," Cloe calls, rattling my leash and collar as I head toward the open door at the front of the barn.

Looking over my shoulder, I pause, so she can catch up

and clasp the collar around my neck. A wave of warm air greets us as we exit the barn. It's going to be hot today. The strip of grass that separates the driveway from Gus's sheep and their fenced pasture is already dry. Cloe lets me squat again and again, which is another reason why I like her so much. This place is overrun with opossums, raccoons, field mice, and at least one skunk at night. It's my responsibility to remind them this place belongs to me during the day.

As I move from one fence post to another, marking my territory, the sheep bleat, causing a terrible racket. When I glance over at them, I notice again how they always huddle together, sort of like puppies in a den. But they're not puppies, and they're not confined to a den. They have an enormous pasture of hills and valleys, and even a little creek to sniff and explore. But they never seem to do much exploring. They seem happy to spend all their time crammed together in a lump of white. If they ever spread out, it's not very far.

The strangest thing of all is how they keep their faces smashed in the grass all the time. I've tried a few blades over the years, and believe me it's nothing to get excited about. But something about it must appeal to certain animals. Diana certainly loved her plants.

Shaking my head, I huff just above the grass to stir up the scent of what appears to be a young coyote. My long ears catch the odor and channel it back down to my nose.

I'm so focused on my find, I don't see or hear Nando and Esperanza until they're almost on top of us.

"If you want to go inside, you can bring a travel crate out here for Stella," Esperanza says. "She can watch Nando and me work if you want to read, or call someone to play or something."

Lifting my ears, I swivel my head back and forth from Esperanza to Cloe, trying to understand their words.

"I'll stay with Stella. She probably doesn't want to go back in her crate so soon."

I lift the whiskers above my eyes, trying to show my sadness at the word *crate*.

Cloe smiles at me as if she understands. "Let's sit in the shade and watch," she says, leading me toward an enormous tree outside the pasture.

Esperanza slaps her thigh, and Nando falls in beside her. They weave through an enormous swinging gate. Nando's tail hangs low, his eyes focused directly on the sheep. His head droops below his shoulders. The tips of both ears point toward the sheep, on high alert, but one rotates back and forth from the sheep to Esperanza, again and again.

Gus rises from the grass on his long legs but makes no effort to greet us. He watches with old, black eyes that seem to take in information the way my nose does—sort of just soaking it up. When I turn back to the sheep, they're clumped so close together, I can't tell where one begins and the next ends. Their bleating rings in my ears, drowning out the birds and insects and every other sound on the farm. The sheep seem afraid of Nando, which I don't understand since they do this every day, and he's never hurt them before.

Cloe rubs my ears as we watch to see what will happen next. I push into the pressure of her hand and sigh. When her hand travels to the top of my head and down the back of my neck, my eyes close a little. I'm not chasing rabbits or watching the sheep or searching the airport, but I think this might be just as good.

Cloe's heart beats evenly. She smells more like bacon and books than the sour vinegar smell that sometimes seeps from her body. When her fingers pause underneath the collar circling my neck, I stretch my nose to the sky, trying to make more room for her to reach all the itchiest spots.

"Oh, girl, this is too tight." She slides her fingers free, and I open my eyes to see what could have caused her to stop something that felt so unbelievably good. She smells okay and looks okay as she unclasps my collar.

"Let me adjust that." Her forehead wrinkles as she tugs at the clasps and buckles.

Just then, Esperanza whistles, and Nando runs up the hill behind Gus and away from the sheep. I glance at

Esperanza, trying to figure out why Nando is running *away* from the sheep, but before I can make sense of the strange maneuver, he makes a big loop and approaches them from above and behind. The sheep move away from him in one liquid motion.

"Come-bye," Esperanza shouts, lifting one arm to the sky.

Nando pivots on his back legs, changing directions faster than a squirrel with an acorn. And so do the sheep. My ears lift. I wag my tail. This is starting to look like a game of chase-the-rabbits, except the sheep are way bigger and Nando is way faster. My back legs quiver at the possibility, ready to push through the brushy grass at top speed. I really want to give it a try. But I concentrate on sitting still and showing Cloe what a good dog I am, even though my collar is off and I am very tempted to run, run, run.

My eyes dart in the direction of one of the smaller sheep as it breaks from the flock. Nando races forward, head and shoulders low, eyes trained on its back feet. The sheep dashes back to the group, and Nando scans the field for other runaways.

"Atta, boy!" Esperanza shouts. "Yes! Yes! Yes!"

She is making a very big deal of Nando's game of chase. Surely, she knows *all* dogs are good at chase. Maybe Esperanza would see what a good dog I am if I chase the sheep too. She might trust me enough to leave me out of the crate at night. Suddenly, it seems very important that I show Esperanza and Cloe how good I am at chase. They seem to have forgotten all about me.

Cloe is still fussing with my collar. Esperanza is *oohing* and *aahing* over Nando. No one actually gave me a command, but no one said *stay* either. So I decide to show off.

I'm a good chaser. I know how important it is to time my advance and how important it is to study the movements of the sheep. I'm so good I even study Nando and Gus to see how their positions might affect my charge.

"That'll do," Esperanza says, and Nando backs away from the sheep a little. Gus steps forward quietly. The sheep clump together like always.

"Can you get the gate, Cloe? I'm going to move them to the back pasture." Esperanza speaks calmly and quietly like she doesn't want to upset the sheep, who still smell nervous even though they're just standing there, doing nothing.

Cloe nods and stands. And I realize something is getting ready to happen. I'm going to miss my opportunity to chase if I don't do something *now*. So I run toward the fence, duck my head under the bottom rail, and enter the pasture. Nando yaps at me, serious as usual. The pool of sheep retreat a couple of steps, somehow contracting into an even tighter ball.

"No!" Cloe shouts, jumping to her feet.

I'm thankful Cloe is on my side and shouting at the sheep, but she doesn't need to tell them to be still for me. I've got the situation under control. I'm an expert at chase and ready to show everyone it can be way more fun if they do it my way. So I wag my tail, lift my head, and spring toward the sheep. They break into two groups, like water flowing around a rock, which is pretty spectacular. Now Nando and I can each have a group of our own. Thankful the sheep are finally trying something new, I tilt my head to the sky and let loose a full-on yowl.

Esperanza whistles loudly. Nando darts one way, then the other. Gus moves forward, and the two of them have their half of the sheep clumped together again in no time, which is boring. I decide to try something new and run straight for the middle of my group.

When the sheep scatter like kibble dropped on a hard floor, I can hardly believe my luck. In no time, the pads of my feet warm, and my tongue lolls out the side of my mouth. I chase one sheep and then another just the way I would kibble on a slippery floor.

"No! No! No!" Esperanza shouts, running toward my group of sheep and waving her arms.

Cloe waves her arms around excitedly, too, and I realize she wants to play as well.

So I race back to the humans, yapping and bouncing

around their feet, then fly back to the sheep, who are already falling back into their typical clumpy formation.

Out of the corner of my eye, I see Esperanza step into a dip in the ground and lose her balance. A second later, she lands in the grass on her behind with a grumpy-sounding harrumph. She looks very, very angry.

Cloe freezes, her mouth hanging open as she glances from the sheep, to me, to her mom. Neither of them moves.

I wag my tail, wondering if they're ready to get back to our game.

Cloe's face breaks into a smile, but she doesn't run or shout. Esperanza bites down on her lower lip with her teeth but doesn't get up to play. So I run to her, stand on my back legs, and lick her face. She still doesn't get up, but she does laugh. And it's one of those human laughs that comes from way down deep in the belly.

Cloe walks over and offers a hand to Esperanza, who accepts it and pulls herself to her feet.

"I'm glad no one was here to see that," Esperanza says as she brushes grass from the seat of her pants.

"It was pretty funny." Cloe leans down, clasping the collar around my neck.

I'm pretty sure that means we're done with chase-the-sheep. It's a good thing I jumped in when I did, or they would have missed the fun.

"Atta, boy, Nando," Esperanza says, nodding to Nando

then turning back to Cloe. "Funny to us. Not to the sheep. They're our livelihood, and it's almost shearing season. This probably wasn't the best time for me to take in a dog that needs a lot of special attention." She sounds tired and discouraged.

When I glance at Cloe, her face is all pinched together too, and I wonder yet again how human moods can change so quickly. We were just playing chase and having fun. Cloe and Esperanza were laughing. Now, they look like someone stole their favorite toy and forgot to feed them.

I sit in the grass, staring up at them, waiting for them to remember me and tell me what an excellent chaser I am— what a good girl I am.

But that doesn't happen. What does happen is Cloe clips the leash to my collar and leads me back to the barn for a very long, very boring afternoon in my crate.

Chapter Seven

A few evenings later, Esperanza leads me up the hill to the field behind the barn. Cloe follows close behind, her feet scuffing the dry dirt. The sun dips beneath the tree line but does nothing to lessen the sweltering heat. With my belly full, I'm content to lie in the grass under a nearby tree as Esperanza and Cloe scatter cardboard boxes around one end of the field.

"It's time to get Stella back to work," Esperanza says as she nudges one of the boxes with her toe.

"What do the boxes have to do with work?" Cloe asks. Thanks to a ribbon securing her long, dark hair, I have a good view of her eyes as she watches her mother.

"We need to start with something she's good at, like scent work. After that fiasco with the sheep the other day,

I think she's bored. She needs a job, but I don't think she's ready for the stress of obedience or agility."

A breath of warm air whispers through the trees. Tilting my head back, I savor the brush of the wind on my whiskers and the feel of my ears falling away from my face and fluttering on the breeze. My eyes grow heavy as Esperanza and Cloe continue talking and laying out one box after another. Sniffing through one nostril and then the other, I half-heartedly zero in on a squirrel in a nearby tree.

Then something slaps the ground beside my face, and I yelp. Jumping to my feet, I scan the area for danger. My heart jumps, too, pounding in my chest before I realize it's just one of Esperanza's boxes, carried farther than she intended by the wind.

"Poor baby," Cloe says, stepping toward me and leaning down, ready to pick me up.

"No." Esperanza stops her. "We can't baby her. That just encourages the fear and anxiety."

"But you said this was supposed to be fun, like a game." Cloe twists her long hair around her fingers as she glances back and forth between me and Esperanza. "She doesn't look like she's having fun."

"Here. Take the leash." Esperanza plucks my leash from the dirt and hands it to Cloe. "Turn her away so she can't see what I'm doing."

Cloe walks me back to the edge of the woods where

we stand facing the trees. She rubs my chin as Esperanza shuffles around behind us.

"I'm going to hide a piece of leftover enchilada in one of the boxes. All she has to do is find it. We brag on her, then increase the difficulty a little each time until she really has to work to find it."

"Okay," Cloe says, but she smells uncertain.

"Being successful will build her confidence and help us bond with her. Then we can move on to obedience or agility, or whatever you want. Now, turn her around," Esperanza commands. "We don't have much time before dark."

We turn to face the boxes. The setting sun casts swaying shadows around the field. Esperanza peers at the strap on her wrist. She smells tense.

"Unclip the leash. And tell her to search."

My nose twitches. A perfume of meat and flour floats toward me on the breeze from inside the noisy box that slapped the ground.

Cloe smiles and unclips my leash. "Search," she says.

I sit with my behind planted in the sand beside her. That box may smell good, but I'm not sure it's worth the effort after the sound it made. And if they want me to do *find it*, they're doing it all wrong. I wear a harness when I do *find it*. I have Connie when I do *find it*.

Looking up at Cloe, I whine for help. When she doesn't

move, I wag my tail, hoping maybe she'll retrieve the yummy goodness from the box for me.

"Do not look at her," Esperanza says. "She needs to know the game is out here in the boxes. It's about her being independent—not about her relying on you. She'll get it."

I whine again then paw Cloe's foot.

"Don't look at her," Esperanza says again as she steps closer to the suspicious-sounding box with the yummy smell.

My ears sag. My eyes droop. I cannot do what they want me to do.

"Search," Cloe says, clapping her hands together, like this is supposed to be fun.

When I glance up at her again, she smiles and points toward the boxes. Despite how wrong it feels to be searching without a harness and without Connie, I take one small step toward the first box.

"Yes!" Cloe and Esperanza cheer and lightly clap their hands.

My tail wags weakly as I take another step. Then an explosion splits the air. I freeze. My collar feels tight. I can't breathe. My head darts back and forth. I'm disoriented by the ringing in my ears, like that day at the airport.

"Ugh!" Esperanza lifts a fist to the sky. "That Vern and his stupid guns are going to be the death of me."

Cloe quietly lowers herself to the sand and pulls me

into her lap. The heat from her body warms the pads of my feet. The panting grips me, but I don't struggle to free myself. I can't. My claws might scratch Cloe. Instead, I curl into her chest and try to make myself smaller.

"Of all the bad timing. If that man were half as considerate about our animals as he wants everyone to be about his garden, I might respect him." She starts collecting boxes, stacking them one inside of the other. "Let's pack it in for the night. I'll start fresh with her tomorrow."

"I thought tomorrow was the day those guys are coming to help shear the sheep." Cloe runs her hand from the top of my head, down my neck and back, to the tip of my tail.

Esperanza's shoulders drop, like a heavy weight is bearing down on her. "Oh, yes, it is. I don't know what's wrong with me."

"You're busy. I could work Stella, so you can focus on the sheep. She likes me." She rubs her cheek on the top of my head, her heart beating against my side.

I sigh and lick her chin, trying to show her how much I appreciate her help.

"I don't want you to get too attached. I don't think it's a good idea—"

"I've helped with other dogs."

"But they were dogs that had owners. You knew they

were leaving when you started working with them. I'm just afraid—"

"We'll play games and go on walks. Please. Let me try it for a few weeks. You were training dogs with Abuelo when you were twelve."

The firm line of Esperanza's jaw relaxes. She places a stack of boxes on the ground then comes to sit with us. Esperanza drapes an arm across Cloe's shoulders then reaches to scratch the back of my head. The three of us sit together quietly as the tree frogs and crickets tune up for the evening. A firefly blinks at the edge of the woods, then another, and another. I stay very, very still, pressed against Cloe's chest, wanting to stay just like this.

I'm not sure what just happened between these two or what it has to do with me. But I'm pretty sure things are getting ready to change again.

Chapter Eight

Later in the week, clouds roll into the valley, but they do nothing to relieve the heat. In fact, they hold the hot, moist air closer to the ground, almost like a blanket. The mornings are still nice enough, though, and the clouds keep all the good smells close to the ground where I can drink them in and enjoy every little detail, including the slugs the opossums ate for dinner last night.

Thankfully, Cloe has been arriving earlier and earlier in the morning. Ever since the evening with the boxes, she spends more time with me, and Esperanza spends more time with the sheep.

"Rise and shine, Stella Bella," she says, the heavy barn door rumbling as she rolls it to the side. Nando trots out of the feed room to greet her. Standing, I rattle the door on the front of the crate with my toenails.

"It's breakfast time!" she calls in a singsong voice as she clanks my and Nando's metal bowls together.

My mouth floods with water as I wait for her to appear.

When she turns the corner and climbs the large step to the feed room, Nando is glued to her lower leg. It's the first time I sort of dislike Nando. I really, really want to sleep out in the open barn without a crate and wander around inside the barn if I feel like it. I want to follow Cloe from place to place and stick close to her leg.

I wag my tail at the lovely cloud scent surrounding her this morning. I've always enjoyed the smell of grass, books, and cookies. Now, I'm learning to enjoy the sharp, unique Cloe smell that I have no name for. Some days it's stronger than others. Today, as she places the two bowls on top of my crate, it's barely recognizable—hidden under many other smells, including the peppers and onions she had with her eggs this morning. Nando watches her with his intense eyes as she opens the front of my crate.

As soon as the door swings open, I rush forward, bouncing in circles around her feet. Nando looks down his serious nose at me, but I don't care. It feels good to be free. Esperanza and Cloe have excellent taste in dog food. And Cloe and I might explore the forest again today, which is cooler than the farm and filled with fresh smells that make my nostrils practically vibrate.

To top it all off, Cloe places my bowl on the floor first.

That means I'm her favorite dog and shows Nando that I'm important too, even if I don't have a job like him or Gus. When Cloe reaches inside a big cabinet, metal tags clink and clank. I lift my ears but keep my face firmly in my bowl until I've gobbled up every last crumb of the tasty meal.

When I turn to her, she's smiling, and my leash and collar dangle from her hand. My toenails click out a joyful noise on the wood floor as I scamper to her feet. My butt smacks the ground, and I sit attentively with my head tilted back for a good view of her face. The pack fastened around her middle holds something that smells like moist chicken livers.

"You want to play, Stella?" she asks, leaning down and clipping the collar around my neck.

Yes. Yes. Yes, I want to play. *Play* means run and chase and sometimes treats. I glance at the delicious-smelling pouch she wears at her waist.

I look over at Nando to see if he's as excited as I am to go outside and play, but he's still eating. I've never seen a dog eat so slowly. It's like he's thinking even when he's eating.

"Let's go potty first," Cloe says as we head out to the gravelly road. When I do my business quickly, she says, "Good, girl! Treat."

Then she reaches into the pouch around her middle and tosses me a little ball of meaty goodness. My nose was right—it's chicken and liver and maybe even pepperoni all mashed together. If playing is going to involve what's in that pouch, it's going to be a very, very fun day.

The treat is so distractingly delicious that I don't see or hear Esperanza until she calls out to us. "What are you girls up to so early this morning?" she asks, her rubber boots leaving tracks in the dew-covered grass as she walks toward us.

Cloe shrugs. "I thought we'd play some games."

Esperanza pauses to greet Nando, who's rocketing toward her as fast as an airplane. I watch, positive he's going to slam into her legs, but somehow, he stops just in time to bounce, spin, tear past her, and come in for a second approach. She ruffles the fur near his face with one hand but doesn't stop walking.

"Easy, Nando," she says calmly but firmly, and it's like someone flipped a light switch. He goes from jumping-rabbit-dog to intense-working-dog in an instant. "Isn't today the day you're supposed to check out that summer writing group at the library?"

I watch Esperanza's face as she speaks to Cloe. Her words lift at the end, which usually means hopeful or happy, or both. Her mouth smiles, but the smile doesn't reach her eyes. I tilt my head and wag my tail, trying to make the smile reach her eyes.

"I think I'd rather stay home with Stella today." Cloe's

hand rustles inside the food pouch at her waist, and I lick my lips.

"You can't sit home alone all summer," Esperanza says as she gently tugs on Nando's ear.

"I'm not alone, Mama. I've got Stella, and you said she needs lots of help. And you said playing builds a bond between dog and trainer. I thought it would be a good thing."

"Yes, I did say that. And it is a good thing but—"

"And you said it builds confidence in the dog," Cloe says, maintaining eye contact with her mother. For such a small girl, she sounds like she thinks she could be the top human someday. "You said it builds confidence in humans too."

"Yes, I did." Esperanza's lips wiggle as if she's holding back a real smile, which is something I'll never understand about humans.

Dogs don't hold back smiles. When a dog wants to smile, she smiles. There is no shame in stretching your lips back to your ears or even in letting your tongue hang out.

Cloe crosses her arms and doesn't back down. "She's doing a lot better. She barely even jumped when the helicopter flew over yesterday. Training a little can't hurt her, right?"

"No, it can't hurt her. I just don't want to see *you* get hurt if things don't work out. And I think it would be good for you to have human friends as well."

"I won't get hurt, Mama. I promise. I can handle it. I'm practically twelve. And I have friends at school. I don't need them over the summer." Cloe lifts her chin and shoulders, stretching to her full height, like a dog defending a bone.

"You are growing up, and sounding pretty confident too—" Nando rudely nudges his head under Esperanza's hand, as if she could have forgotten him there, attached to her lower body like a third leg. She rubs his head as she continues. "Speaking of growing up, did you remember to take your medicine this morning?"

"Yes. I always do."

"Yes, you do, and I'm very thankful." Esperanza brushes Cloe's cheek with her hand. Then turning away from Nando, she kneels down in front of me and scratches me under the chin. Nando huffs when she speaks to me. "Connie said you were the best dog on the planet, Stella Bella. So prove it."

I whimper at the sound of Connie's name.

"Who's Connie?" asks Cloe.

"She was a friend of mine from college and an amazing dog woman. She was Stella's handler."

"The one who . . ."

"Yes." Esperanza nods but doesn't forget to scratch the back of my head when she talks. "I haven't seen her in years, but I read about the accident and called her work to find out about the funeral. When they realized I was a trainer, they asked me to come in and test a few dogs for them. Stella was being returned by her third owner that day. One thing led to another, and here we are."

"I'm glad she's here." Cloe smiles down at me.

All their attention and kindness is almost as good as the treats in Cloe's pouch.

Esperanza tousles my ears then stands. "Me too, and I'm really glad you want to work with her. Y'all have fun. Check in with me at lunch, okay?"

"We will. Let's go, Stella!" Cloe slaps her thigh just like Connie used to do. It's a command I know, and I'm happy to follow, especially if it means I might have a chance at more of those good, meaty treats.

We spend much of the morning in the field of sand practicing tricks. The first trick confuses me a bit.

Cloe repeats over and over, "Watch me. Watch me."

I don't understand what she wants me to do. I glance around at different pieces of the play equipment in the field, wondering if this trick has something to do with the horrid teeter-totter, but she doesn't move or point at any of the obstacles. Instead, she reaches into her pouch and brings out a piece of meat. My mouth waters as she rolls the treat into a bite-sized ball. My eyes lock on the lump of deliciousness. When she lifts her hand, I fear she's going to devour the treat right in front of me, but she doesn't.

Instead, she places it near her face and says, "Watch me."

I look her straight in the eye, begging her to share it with me.

The second our eyes lock, she says, "Treat!"

Then she tosses me the food. It seems almost too easy. But we keep playing, and it works every time.

Cloe says, "Watch me."

I look into her eyes, which is a little strange for a dog, but not too uncomfortable with a kind human.

Every time we connect eye-to-eye, she says, "Treat!"

And I get the meaty reward. I like this game—very much. We play other games too, like *touch*, which basically means she wants me to touch my nose to a round rubber target she keeps placing at farther and farther distances across the field. I like this game too. Even the *leave it* game, which is sort of odd, is fun. In this game, I pretend I'm not interested in the food in her hand. And if I pretend I'm not interested for long enough, she gives me the food. Every. Single. Time.

But the *watch me* game is my favorite. The more I look into her eyes, the more I like it. She has really kind, really big, dark eyes, like my mother's.

We're trying a new version of *watch me* where we walk side-by-side across the field, when Esperanza's voice interrupts our practice.

"Time to eat," she calls from the direction of the house.

My ears perk up at the word *eat*. I love how two of my favorite words sound so much alike—*eat* and *treat*. The possibility of even more food seems almost too good to be true—too much for one beagle to hope for. But I put an extra spring in my step as we descend the gravelly hill and head toward the house, just in case.

Today has been a good day—a very good day. And it's not even over yet.

The sun breaks through the clouds. A whiff of a breeze tickles my whiskers. As we approach the little house in the shadows, I tell myself nothing bad can happen on a day like today. Bad things don't happen to nice humans on nice farms hidden away from the airport and protected on all sides by towering mountains.

Bad things happen far, far away from here. That's what I keep telling myself anyway.

Because that's what I really, really want to believe.

Chapter Nine

As the days pass, the temperature rises higher and higher. Water falls from the sky less and less often. Even though I know Connie's not coming back, I still miss her. I miss the sound of her strong voice. I even miss the smell of the bitter beans and hot water that she and Jake drank in the morning at the canine facility when they shared words back and forth.

Sometimes, my stomach aches with missing her, and I whimper. But the ache isn't constant. Sometimes, I'm so busy playing *watch me* or *touch* with Cloe that my stomach forgets to ache. Other times, the ache comes on in a sudden crash—like the other day when a tall woman with short hair visited the farm. Her small car rattled like Connie's. The woman even wore clothes like Connie's with metal objects clipped to her belt and patches with designs attached to the sleeves.

I wagged my tail and trotted toward her. Then the wind shifted in my direction, blowing the woman's scent to me, and I knew instantly the woman wasn't Connie.

But last night, I slept through the night without waking in fear. I can't remember the last time I bloodied my nose or paws trying to dig out of anything, and I haven't chewed any wood or blankets in a long time.

If the uncomfortable heat and dying grass are the worst that can happen, I won't complain. There are dogs with no humans, dogs living on the street, and dogs who spend their entire lives behind fences, or worse, on chains. And there are lots and lots of dogs sniffing for bad chemicals in airports every day. I know because Connie and I often went to different airports and showed other dogs and their humans how to sniff the largest areas in the shortest amount of time.

And the hot weather has at least one benefit. It seems to relieve some of my fear, the way a heating pad relaxed the muscles in Connie's back after a long day on her feet at the airport.

Today should be a good day too. We're taking a car ride—not in the big vehicle with the sliding doors. Esperanza has another car, a smaller one, a lot like Connie's. And I get to ride in the front seat. On Cloe's lap. And I'm the only dog in the car. Nando had to stay in the barn, and Gus had to stay where he always stays, in the field with his sheep.

As we drive away from the farm, Cloe rolls down the window, allowing me to step on the door handle and poke my head out. My ears flap in the wind. My nose tingles from all the new smells. There's a creek somewhere in the forest near the road, and lots of deer and rabbits.

"Look how happy she is, Mama," Cloe says as she runs a hand down my back.

"Mm-hmm." Esperanza keeps her eyes on the road and taps on the wheel with her thumbs. "You're doing a really good job with her."

"She was already trained though."

"Don't underestimate yourself, Cloe. She may have been trained for scent work, but you're teaching her entirely new skills. And she came to us with serious problems that some dog trainers could never cure."

It's hard to understand why humans speak so many words. I wish I could tell them how much faster and easier they could gather information with their noses.

"I'll cure her," Cloe says as I twist my head back and forth, zeroing in on the smell of food places, traffic, and strangers building in the distance.

Esperanza glances away from the winding black road unrolling like a length of rope in front of us, her mouth straight and firm. "Cloe, please. It's way too early to be certain. We'll have to try her in lots of stressful situations before we'll know for sure if her improvement is far-reaching and permanent."

"Just watch her today. You'll see." Cloe grasps and wiggles the loose skin on the back of my neck.

We work our way down the mountain, stopping at many places—none of them food places—spending most of the morning getting in and out of the car. We drop off papers at one building and pick up papers at another. We even drop some of Cloe's books into a large metal container with a swinging door that looks and sounds very heavy. The special trash can is attached to a brick building with a flag waving out front and seems to be just for books. Cocking my head, I glance from Cloe's face to the trash can, then back to Cloe's face. She isn't sad about throwing away the books she loves so much. So I go back to gathering information with my nose.

"Why don't we go in and sign up for a summer reading book club? You might meet some nice kids."

"I'm good, Mama. I'd rather choose my own books."

"Then why don't we go check out some new ones?" Esperanza asks.

"No. I think I'm going to reread some of my favorites to Stella."

I lift one ear at the sound of my name then go back to twitching my nose as they exchange words back and forth, back and forth. We're passing Connie's favorite food place—the one that slips a piece of meat between pieces of bread with little seeds on top. But Esperanza doesn't stop.

"Let me guess. Harry Potter?" she asks as she drives away from the delicious place. It's like she doesn't even smell it.

Cloe shakes her head. "I have something I think Stella will like better."

"Better than Harry Potter?"

"Yep."

"Percy Jackson?" Esperanza turns the wheel, and the car stops near a building that doesn't smell like food or books or anything very wonderful.

"Not even close," Cloe says.

"Well, then, what do you think a bomb-sniffing dog will want to read?"

"I thought I'd start with *Charlotte's Web*," Cloe says, snapping my leash to my collar and opening the door.

"That's always a good choice—but sad."

"I think Stella can handle it, Mama," Cloe says.

Heat rises from the pavement as we approach the store, but I don't let that stop me from sniffing. A big dog has been here ahead of us, and I wonder if this is the store Connie used to take me to with fish and birds and rows and rows of dog food. Curious, I pull toward the large sliding door.

But as soon as the doors open, I know there are no interesting animals and no rows and rows of dog food.

This store is all slick floors—no carpet or grass anywhere. In place of squeaky toys and rawhides, it has rows and rows of shovels, wheelbarrows, and other tools that don't smell very good. About the most interesting odors in the whole place drift from bags of soil and tree bark and what might be bags of horse manure. I'll never understand why humans keep their carpet so clean, but they gather piles and piles of the stuff chickens and horses squat out of their behinds, mix it with dirt, and then spread it all over their yards.

Despite the lack of interesting smells, I keep my nose to the ground. Humans sometimes drop food in the most unusual places. As I sniff for a dropped bit of meat, an enormous man stops me in my tracks with a loud laugh. The hair on my back bristles.

"You hunting rabbits now, Esperanza?" he asks.

My head snaps to attention. Rabbits? I don't smell rabbits.

"No, Vern—just a new dog we're training," Esperanza says, her jaw tightening when she speaks.

"You can't train hounds—too stubborn." The man peers into her eyes, like they're in a serious game of *watch me*. "And not too bright."

"Well, everyone's entitled to an opinion. Hope you have a good day." She nods and moves to step around him.

"This hound is smart," Cloe says in a grown-up-sounding voice, and both adults turn their heads toward her. "This is a working beagle. She sniffs for explosives."

"What's she doing here then? I don't remember any bombs in Asheville. Fireworks, maybe." The man smells sour, like old meat, and beneath that lies a faint trace of gunpowder.

"She's here because—"

Esperanza places a hand on Cloe's arm. "She's here for agility training."

The man's stomach rises and falls when he laughs. "Agility. Dogs aren't meant to do tricks. They're meant to work—guard, hunt, retrieve. You should let me train the hound."

Esperanza moves her hand from Cloe's arm to her back then gently pulls on my leash with the other. "Thanks, Vern, but we've got it under control. We'll see you around."

We head up the aisle toward stacks of cut-up wood and away from the towering man, but his voice follows us.

"Hounds will break your heart every time. They're more loyal to their noses than their handlers. You may think you've trained her, that you can trust her off leash, but give her one scent of a squirrel, and she'll forget she ever knew you."

73

When Esperanza and Cloe ignore him and keep on moving, I take that as my signal to go back to sniffing the floor for food. Unlike the animal store, there is nothing of interest underneath any of these shelves. Esperanza and Cloe are silent as they explore the next row. Without their voices to listen to, I pay closer attention to their movements.

Esperanza moves in her normal way, but something is different about Cloe. It's not so much her movement that's strange. It's more in the way she smells. The chemical odor that's always a part of Cloe grows stronger and stronger as we head to the front of the store with Esperanza's supplies.

We're almost to the beeping machine with the moving shelf when the large man with the large voice appears again.

"Don't forget the nephews are here until the Fourth, Esperanza. They might be hunting squirrels and whatnot. Make sure your dogs stay off my land."

Something about the way his face pinches in on itself when he speaks to Esperanza raises my hackles.

Cloe opens her mouth, but before she can speak, Esperanza says, "My dogs don't go on your land, Vern."

"It's hard to tell where one property ends and the other begins. And there was that mutt of yours that ruined my okra last summer."

"The property line's where it's always been—right at the creek. And that *mutt* didn't belong to me." Esperanza's eyes narrow. "You make sure your nephews stay off our land."

The man opens his mouth to speak then seems to change his mind and walks away. I'm thankful to be rid of him. Now, maybe I can help Esperanza focus more closely on Cloe. Sitting up straight with my ears raised and my mouth open a little, I try to tell Esperanza that Cloe's chemical smell is getting stronger—that something is wrong. But she doesn't know the *find-it-and-alert* game, or she's too distracted.

I whimper as Esperanza places her items on the moving shelf. Cloe stares out the front doors. Her eyes are far away, not at all like when we play *watch me*.

"You think it's ever going to rain?" the woman in the vest behind the moving shelf asks as she takes some crinkly paper from Esperanza's hand.

Whatever they're doing must be very important because humans really like their crinkly paper, almost as much as they like their words and their carpet. Esperanza is giving lots of crinkly paper to the woman.

"Let's hope so. I'm worried about my sheep in this heat. I'm having to work the dogs early in the morning or late at night. If the weather doesn't break soon, I'm not sure if I'll be able to work them at all."

"Did you know we're under a forest fire warning?" The

woman points to a paper sticking to the wall beside her beeping machine.

"No, but I can believe it." Esperanza thanks the woman and collects her bags. Then we head out to the car.

Cloe still doesn't look at me. Her eyes stare straight ahead—like she's looking at something but not really seeing anything. And the smell coming off her overpowers everything else in the air around us.

I whimper again and try to lower my behind, but I can't quite sit to alert with the leash wrapped in Cloe's small fist, tugging me forward.

"You're fine, Stella. Come on. Nothing to be nervous about here." Esperanza walks toward the car without looking at me or Cloe.

I look at Cloe's face, wishing Esperanza knew the *watch me* game and would look at Cloe's face too. Can't she smell the chemicals on Cloe? She's way too busy placing her supplies in the back of the car.

After she closes the back door, Esperanza opens the front then starts to slide in behind the wheel. When Cloe doesn't join her, she finally comes back around to look at Cloe.

If Esperanza doesn't do something soon, something bad is going to happen. I know it. The chemicals are so strong. The sharp, sour smell is leaking from Cloe's body. When I bark and spin in a circle, the leash falls from Cloe's hand and slaps the ground. I try the *find-it-and-alert* game again.

"What in the world is wrong with you, Stella?" Esperanza looks at me, then Cloe, then the loose leash snaked around Cloe's feet. Her face tightens. She knows. She knows. Finally, she knows something is wrong with Cloe.

And Esperanza is a top human. She'll know exactly what to do.

When she reaches for Cloe's arm, I wag my tail in relief.

Then Cloe's legs bend like she's going to sit down, but there isn't anywhere for her to sit. I scoot near her. If she'll look at me, maybe the blank look on her face will go away, and my Cloe will come back.

But Cloe doesn't look at me. She doesn't come back to me.

She crumples in a silent lump on the hard pavement. I whine and nuzzle her cold fingers, really, really hoping her smell doesn't change to the outside-of-a-human smell. I do not want anyone putting my new friend in a box.

Chapter Ten

Ignoring the hot pavement scalding my belly, I lie in the down position and stretch my legs stick-straight in front of my face. With my haunches tucked under my behind, I turn my head back and forth from Cloe to Esperanza. I want to do *something* but don't know what to do. Esperanza glances at the strap around her wrist then grabs a blanket from the back of the car and places it under Cloe's head.

Cloe's arms jerk and twitch. Her head shakes as she stares blankly at the sky. When I inch closer to her, one of her flopping arms swats my neck. I don't care. I want to be close to her in case there's something—anything—I can do to help.

Esperanza's forehead wrinkles as she speaks quiet words into Cloe's ear. As she gently brushes Cloe's cheek, she checks the strap on her arm again and again.

The tip-tap of approaching footsteps distracts me for a second, and I glance over my shoulder. A tiny woman with a sagging face scurries toward us, balancing a pot of flowers in each hand. "Oh, my! Are you okay? Can I help?"

I whine, thankful another human is here.

"I think we're okay," Esperanza says without taking her eyes or hands off Cloe's face. "She has epilepsy."

"Should I call an ambulance?" The woman's voice rises as she speaks. She shifts one pot to the crook of the opposite arm then digs around in a bag hanging from her shoulder.

"Not unless it lasts more than five minutes." Esperanza practically ignores the woman. The side of her face tightens when she glances at the strap on her wrist again then brushes another lock of dark hair away from Cloe's eyes and mouth. "Cloe, I'm here, baby. You're okay. I've got you."

Then just as suddenly as Cloe fell to the ground, she stops moving. I look at Esperanza, hoping she will fix what is wrong. Cloe should be up—laughing, walking, or looking at a book. She shouldn't be motionless like a rock on the hot ground. I try to stay still—to be quiet. But it's getting harder, and my rear end wiggles, despite my determination to be a good dog.

If Cloe had a wound, I would lick it, but I don't smell any bleeding or bruising. So I try even harder not to move, and I wait for Esperanza to guide me the way Connie always did. But all Esperanza does is grasp Cloe's hands in her own and continue whispering.

When Cloe's eyelids flutter, I let the cry I've been holding back escape my open mouth. It seems like the chemicals swelling and leaking from Cloe's body are beginning to fade. But she still isn't coming back to me. She's still just lying there. I doubt it will do any good, but I wiggle on my belly toward her anyway. Scooting in close enough to lick her hand, I try to tell her it will be okay with my tongue.

My loose leash twists behind me on the pavement, but I make no effort to run. I would never leave Cloe when she needed a friend. I'll stay here all day—until the sun sets and the pavement cools—if I have to.

Esperanza reaches down and pats my head without taking her eyes off of Cloe. "Good girl, Stella. Good girl," she says.

But I don't feel very good. I knew the bad smell was growing and that something bad was going to happen, and I didn't protect Cloe or do anything to help. All I did was watch. I did sit quietly without causing trouble, but any dog could have done that. All of a sudden, I realize I don't just want to be good anymore. I want to be brave again too—like I used to be with Connie.

But I can't think about that right now because Cloe's eyes are fluttering open. The sharp metal smell coming from her body is starting to fade. Her fingers wiggle, and I inch even closer.

"Stella?" she says, looking around.

I whine and she reaches for me. Her tiny gesture releases the tension coiling like snakes in my back legs.

"Oh, Cloe," Esperanza says, sweat shining on her forehead. One of her hands rests on Cloe's cheek. The other flutters around her own neck like a hummingbird. "That one seemed really long. It scared me."

"I'm sorry, Mama." Cloe's eyelids droop.

I nuzzle my head under her hand, wondering if she notices how her palm is perfectly sized to fit the top of my head. It's almost like we're two pieces of one of the jigsaw puzzles Connie used to put together on the kitchen table.

"Don't be sorry, sweetie," Esperanza says, leaning down and covering Cloe's face with kisses.

Movement catches my eye, and I remember the older woman with the pots. The plants sit on the back of a car parked near ours.

"I got water," she says, offering two bottles to Esperanza.

"Thanks." Esperanza smiles at the little woman. She helps Cloe to her feet then takes one of the bottles, unscrews the cap, and offers it to her.

Cloe shakes her head and slides into the car, looking away from the strangers gathering behind the woman.

"I just want to go home. Okay?" She closes her eyes, resting her head on the back of the seat.

"Of course, sweetie," Esperanza says and clicks the safety belt across Cloe's chest.

When Cloe pats the front seat, I don't hesitate. I crawl into her lap, lick her hand, and tell myself everything will be okay now. Cloe won't get that faraway look in her eyes ever again. She won't get that sharp, metallic smell again. And she definitely won't fall down on the hot ground and thrash around again. Ever.

On the way home, I sit very quietly in her lap without trying to look out the window or sniff, even when we pass the yummy food places.

When the car turns off the smooth road and onto the rocky driveway, I sit up for a better view but move slowly and carefully, so I won't disturb Cloe. She seems tired after all the excitement at the store. As far as I'm concerned, we should not go near that horrible place or that horrible man ever again.

A few minutes later, the house comes into view, and Nando rockets out of the barn toward us in a dark blur. Esperanza stops the car and comes around to open Cloe's door. When Nando rubs Esperanza's leg, she pats his head, but he doesn't nudge her hand or cling to her leg or any-thing, which is totally out of the ordinary.

"Hi, Nando," Cloe says in a quiet voice as she gently

moves me to Esperanza's empty seat then gives me a light kiss and allows Esperanza to lead her away from me and into the house.

It's warm in the car, even parked in the shade. But the windows are down, and Nando sits close by, his head moving back and forth between me and the house. Cloe and Esperanza are wise dog people, so I know they won't leave me out here for long. I will be still. I won't bark or dig or cause any problems. If I'm a very good dog, Esperanza might bring me and Nando into the house when she comes back. I will sit with Cloe. She can rest with her hand on my side, and we will both feel better.

When Esperanza appears a few minutes later, I wag my tail hopefully. But her shoulders sag as she approaches the car. And even though she smiles at me and brushes the top of Nando's head with her hand, she smells sad. Lifting my ears and the whiskers above my eyes, I try to make the cute dog face that humans like so much. We're home now. The boring store is long behind us. The grumpy man is gone. Cloe smells better, and I'm here to take care of her. We should not be sad.

"Come on, Stella," Esperanza says as she opens the door and picks up the leash.

I jump to the rocky driveway, turning toward the house and Cloe, but my leash stops me. Esperanza doesn't seem to understand my tugging on the leash or my wagging tail.

"This way," she says when I turn to look at her. "Cloe needs to rest."

My tail drops from steady wag to full droop as we head to the barn. Nando walks beside us, matching his step to our slow, steady rhythm in a pace I didn't know he was capable of. Other than when he's locked in the barn with me at night or when he's intentionally hunching down to study the sheep, I've only seen him move in two speeds—fast and superfast.

When we enter the feed room, Oscar pretends not to watch from his spot on the counter, but his ears flick in our direction, giving him away.

Esperanza unclips my leash and points at the open crate.

I look past her, faking interest in Oscar, who's opened his eyes to tiny slits. I really do not want to be locked in the crate away from Cloe.

"Kennel up," Esperanza says in her top-human voice.

I tuck my tail, creep inside, then turn to look up at her with my saddest eyes. If Esperanza would look at me, she would see my unhappiness and maybe change her mind about this separation business. But Esperanza isn't looking at me as she slides the locking bar on the front of the crate in place.

"Nando, watch," she says as if I'm one of his sheep.

Before she can get away, I inch forward and nudge the

gate with my nose, trying to tell her that I need to be in the house. With Cloe.

"Be good, Stella. There's nothing to worry about," she says, reaching through the bars to rub my nose before leaving.

Nando sighs then lies down beside the crate. He's not any happier about this turn of events than I am, but he's not going anywhere—not when Esperanza gave him a command—despite how sad and droopy his eyes look. When I wiggle the crate door with my nails, he and Oscar both ignore me. When I don't stop, Nando gives me a firm bark. But I meet his eyes and continue rattling and wiggling. I will not be deterred. I will not be separated from Cloe. I need to check her smell, to be close to her, to make sure she's okay.

So I keep rattling and wiggling. After some time, the skin between my nails and the pads of my paws starts to hurt. I try lying down for a minute and whimpering, hoping Oscar or Nando might try to help. But Nando ignores me, watching the door for Esperanza's return.

When I stand and scratch the floor near the gate, Oscar huffs, stretches, then silently jumps to the floor. I think he's had all of me he can take and that he's going to slip through the door and out of sight. I know how cats are. They avoid anything they don't like, which is almost everything involving dogs. But Oscar doesn't stalk away and disappear. Instead, he tiptoes around Nando and straight to my crate.

I whine, hoping he'll do something to help. All he does is rub his neck on the edge of my crate, look me in the eye, and meow. Cats are very hard to understand, but I think he might feel sorry for me. Or maybe he's trying to help.

Either way, I decide he's an okay cat. He's sitting with me and not ignoring me, and every once in a while he rubs his neck along the corner of the crate where the bar locks in place. I squint and focus on the little bar. It's no longer pushed all the way through the row of loops. It's halfway loose.

I don't move. I don't whine. I don't even twitch my nose. I stay frozen in place, hoping Oscar will keep scratching his neck and chin on the edge of the crate near the sliding bar.

After a bit, he flicks his tail, meows, and turns to leave as if Nando and I were never even there. He's grown bored with me, or the crate, or the world. Or maybe his neck just doesn't itch anymore. It's hard to tell with cats. But it doesn't matter.

I know how the little bar moves now.

I have a plan.

And I don't care if Nando or anyone else tries to stop me.

Chapter Eleven

When I nudge the crate door open and step out into the feed room, Nando turns to face me, his eyes narrow. Esperanza said *watch*. And when Esperanza speaks or whistles or even sneezes, Nando listens. He will do anything to please her, which is why his upper lip snarls a little, warning me to stay put. But I will not stay put. In fact, I try very hard not to growl at him. He has been good to me, but I do not like the way he's zigging and zagging in front of me like I am one of his sheep. I am not a sheep. I am a beagle—a beagle on a very important mission. I really, really don't want to get him in trouble, but I will not be stopped.

Racing in a straight line up the center of the barn, I keep my head down, my tail low, and my eyes trained straight ahead. The big, sliding door up front is open a crack, and

I zip through. A wave of heat and smells invades my nose when I break free. For the first time since Diana's house, I'm off leash and without a human. Somehow, the crunchy grass feels better under my paws when there's no leash attached to my collar.

But I'm not interested in the sheep in the field or the squirrel chittering above me in a tree. I'm not even distracted by the smell of rabbits in the grass beside the driveway. I run so fast the gravel pricks my paws, and my legs burn. Panting, I skip the front steps and leap onto the porch. At the front door, I drop my behind to the floor, sit up straight, and lift my ears. With my tongue hanging from the side of my mouth, I wait for any sign of Esperanza or Cloe.

Nando has followed me and barks frantically, clearly distressed by my behavior. Before I have time to catch my breath, the door swings open, and Esperanza stares down at us. Streaks of watery blackness circle her eyes.

"What in the world?" she asks.

Nando bounces on his back legs and yips excitedly.

"Shh," Esperanza hisses at us, and Nando draws back like he's been swiped at by Oscar.

I retreat as well then catch myself and stand my ground near the steps.

"You guys are supposed to be in the barn. Cloe's asleep." She steps onto the porch, pulling the door shut behind her. I don't want to make her mad, but I can't help it—I tip my head back, mouth to the sky, and howl, calling to Cloe like I would to another hound. She needs to know I'm here for her.

"Hush!" Esperanza points at me, her face pinched. There's a bite to her voice I've never heard before.

I look down, but I stay put. Nando takes another step back, his tail low, clearly not wanting to be part of the trouble I'm causing. Heading away from the door, Esperanza slaps her thigh, signaling for us to follow. I want to be a good dog, but I can't leave. Instead, I hunch low to the ground, scurry to the door, then scratch as if a squirrel is teasing me from the other side. Esperanza steps forward, towering over me. When her hand reaches for my collar, I howl again.

"What in the world has gotten into you, Stella?" she asks, dragging me toward the steps, but I dig my nails in, making it as difficult as possible.

Then a faint voice calls from the other side of the door, and my head lifts. My whole body bounces to life. It's Cloe. Cloe!

And Esperanza hears it too because she releases my collar. Pushing me back with her foot, she opens the door a crack to listen.

"Mama, is that Stella?"

I whimper when I hear Cloe say my name. Darting

through Esperanza's legs, I race toward the sound of her voice. I never thought another human could replace Connie. I never considered having a child as my human. They're small, and their emotions are even more up and down than adults, and their voices are all high-pitched and hard to understand. I never would have chosen to leave Connie, but if I can't have her, maybe I am meant to have another human. A smaller one that smells like cookies and books and sometimes tangy chemicals.

The pressure inside my chest seems to be telling me this is how it's supposed to be—that Cloe is supposed to be my new human. And when a dog finds her human, there's not much anyone can do or say to stop it—other than try to separate them. But I refuse to be separated from Cloe now that I've found her.

I race through a small room with a couch and a TV, then down a narrow hall, and straight to Cloe in the back room. She's in bed, in a comfy nest of blankets and pillows. When she sees me, she smiles.

"Hi, girl," she says and pats the bed, inviting me to join her.

I jump but the bed's too high. So I stand on my back legs and scratch at the blankets.

"Come on, girl," she says, reaching for me.

I jump again, aiming for her outstretched arms, but my

front paws slip off the top of the bed. I slide back to the floor.

"What in the world?" Esperanza asks as she enters the tiny room with Nando slouching behind her. "You're supposed to be resting, and Stella's not supposed to be in the house."

Cloe makes puppy eyes at Esperanza, and I'm super impressed. The droop of the skin beneath her eyes would make even the most serious bassett hound proud.

Esperanza sighs. "Oh, okay. But just for tonight." She bends down to pick me up and place me on Cloe's bed. The lines at the corners of her mouth and eyes soften her entire face. The bite is gone from her voice, and I'm pretty sure she's smiling. Nando looks like he might be smiling too. For the first time since we got home from the bad store earlier today, it seems like we can all agree that I should be with Cloe and that Esperanza shouldn't be mad at any of us.

"Mama, please. Just let Stella be a house dog. You said I could have my own dog someday."

"You know I meant a puppy we selected together. One with a pedigree and a good temperament. And we discussed a golden retriever or a lab—something more . . . dependable."

"What if she passes the Canine Good Citizen Test?" Cloe pulls me to her side. I make a tight circle and snuggle up beside her leg. She curls her arm around me, and once again I'm amazed at how perfectly fitted we are to one another.

"Sweetie, just about any family pet can pass that test. It won't prove that Stella can hold her own alone. And I thought you wanted a dog you could train for agility. You said you might want to try Rally and earn titles for working like a team with a well-trained dog."

"I can train her for agility, Mama."

If I weren't exhausted from all the commotion today, the tone of their voices might be more stressful. But I'm in a bed—a real bed for the first time in ages. And it's warm. And everything smells like Cloe. And my eyes are growing heavy despite Esperanza and Cloe's tense voices.

"Cloe, it's not fair to ask Stella to be something she's not." The bed creaks when Esperanza sits down beside us.

"What if I can get her to finish a basic agility course without using treats? Then can she be my dog?"

"This is silly, Cloe. She's a beagle. She's meant for scent work."

"She can do both, Mama." When Cloe runs her hand down my side, I sigh and release the breath I've been holding. Cloe laughs, and the bed jiggles. I open an eye to see what's so funny. Then Esperanza's lower-pitched laugh joins in. I open the other eye to stare at them. Humans are so interesting. I have no idea how we got from Esperanza's pointing finger and biting voice to snuggling and laughing. But I'm very thankful the confusion is sorted out. I'm finally back where I belong—in a cozy house, in a warm bed, curled up beside Cloe.

Now I can rest—really rest—for the first time in a long while, and Esperanza and Nando can get back to their sheep or papers or whatever it is they need to do. I'll just snuggle Cloe, sleep, and work on being a good house dog for the rest of my life.

Chapter Twelve

A few mornings later, I'm right back where I started—in the crate, in the barn, waiting for Cloe to release me. And I am not happy about it either. I don't blame Cloe. It isn't her fault. I don't even really blame Esperanza. She's so busy with all the work around the farm and cutting mounds and mounds of white fuzz off the sheep that she can't help but be confused sometimes. I need to help her understand that I belong inside the house all the time, not just when Cloe is sick.

Sighing, I twitch my nose to one side, then the other, hoping for a whiff of Cloe. Life would be so much easier if I knew all the human words. It would be nearly perfect if humans could understand everything their noses were trying to tell them.

But that's not likely to happen anytime soon. I've tried

to understand all their words. When I first went to live with Connie, I even tried to form words in my mouth. I would tilt my head to the sky and try to move the back part of my tongue that I use to swallow. No words came though, only a cross between a baying hound and very painful human singing. Connie laughed so hard she doubled over, which was fun. But it did nothing to improve my ability to make human sounds.

And people don't seem to be any better at listening or speaking with their noses. They barely seem to smell the food in front of their faces. They certainly don't smell the coming weather or other animals' feelings.

So I don't know how I'm going to show Cloe and Esperanza how wonderful my nose is or how I can use it to take better care of them. Cloe doesn't need to fall down on the hard pavement ever again. I can tell her when her chemical smells are changing so that we can take a nice rest in her comfy bed until they return to normal.

And we would both sleep through the night better if we had someone to snuggle. I've hardly slept the last few nights—not so much because I'm scared to be alone. Not even because I'm scared that bad men with bad chemicals will hurt me. Now that I have a person to care for, I'm much less scared for myself. Now I'm afraid something will happen to Cloe during the night, and I won't be there to protect her.

Wiggling the front gate of my crate, I contemplate a

second escape. Thanks to Oscar's help with my first break-out, I know how the lock works. But Esperanza has guaran-teed I'll never, ever escape again. She added a whole new level of difficulty to the task by wrapping a thick cord with big hooks at either end around the gate and lock. The only way I'm breaking out is if I grow human thumbs.

It's useless, I know, but I jiggle the gate again any-way, then wait and jiggle, wait and jiggle—over and over. Thankfully, Cloe comes before too long. Her small feet crunch the gravel, and the smell of cookies floats toward the barn long before the big door rumbles open. Nando doesn't bolt to meet her with quite as much energy as usual. The unbearable heat seems to be slowing him down as much as it does the sheep in their heavy white coats.

When Cloe releases me, I dance in circles around her feet, my toenails clicking and clacking a joyful sound on the wood floor of the feed room.

"Good morning, girl." She squats down, kissing the top of my head and flapping my ears back and forth.

Smiling up at her, I lick her nose and snuffle air in the back of my throat, trying to tell her how happy I am to see her and how good she smells.

"You're such a good girl, Stella Bella." She laughs, loses her balance, and plops on her behind like a clumsy puppy.

When she does, I notice the bag strapped to her back and tilt my head for a better sniff. She slips it off her shoulders and places it on the floor in front of a cabinet filled with delicious-smelling bins of dog food. As she's scooping out our morning meal and pouring it into our bowls, I investigate the bag. My tail wags at the scent of books and sandwiches and Cloe's bed. I don't know how her bed fits in the bag with the roast beef and books, but my nose never lies, so she must have figured something out.

I don't have time to solve the scent puzzle right now though. My first priority is devouring the food Cloe lowers in front of me. I empty the bowl in the time it takes Nando to chew and chew and chew one bite of his meal. I observe Cloe's every move. She pours food into Oscar's bowl by the time Nando goes in for a second bite.

Cloe doesn't have the bag of meaty goodness strapped around her waist today, so it must not be a *watch me* or a *touch* playday. It's still going to be a good day, though, because Cloe's pulling my leash and collar from the hook above the crate, and she's smiling.

"Let's go tell Mama we're leaving," she says, lifting her bag and slinging it over her shoulder. The tags on my collar jingle when she clips it around my neck. Bouncing down the center aisle of the barn, I'm so happy to be with this girl I almost forget how much I dislike sleeping in the crate.

Outside, the early morning clouds soften the light that is creeping over the big hills and toward the front of the barn. As we near the pasture, Esperanza whistles from somewhere in the direction of the house. Lifting my head from the fresh scent of field mice in the grass, I twitch my nose to zero in on her. But before I fully inhale, Nando shoots past us like a streak of lightning. I wonder again at his speed and how a dog that moves that quickly and is so driven to chase sheep can take so long to eat his food.

But he's acting like a pup now, clearly not as exhausted by the heat as the sheep are. He bounces and yips in circles around Esperanza. As she walks toward the barn, she manages to ruffle the long hair near his face with one hand while he's in mid-leap. She waves to us with the other.

Cloe cups her hands to her mouth to be heard over Nando's yapping. "We're going to walk to the creek. We'll be home in a little while."

"Have fun. Don't go near the water without me," Esperanza calls.

Cloe's shoulders droop a little. "I never do."

"Did you take your medicine?" Esperanza asks, her voice too serious against the backdrop of a morning painted sky-to-ground in pungent aromas.

"Yes, Mama. I always take my medicine. And I ate all my eggs. I'm full of protein and water. I'll be fine on my own for a short walk. Doctor Jones says it's okay if I have a little alone time." She sounds frustrated, which is out of character. Children aren't usually frustrated with top humans. It's generally the other way around.

"You're right, of course. I just love you so much."
Esperanza steps forward, pulling her in for a hug and kissing the top of her head.

"I love you too, Mama." Cloe wraps her arms around
Esperanza, resting her head against her mother's chest.

I paw Cloe's jeans, reminding her I'm down here and
that dogs need hugs too. They laugh and drop their arms.
Tilting my head up at them, I open my mouth a little and
pull my lips into a happy face. This beautifully fragrant
morning is no time to be frustrated. When I tug on the
leash, Cloe gives Esperanza a quick kiss on the cheek and
follows me.

"We won't be gone long," she says over her shoulder.

"What's in the bag?" Esperanza asks, and we stop again.

"Treats and a book. And a blanket. We can't go to the
creek without a few minutes to sit and read."

"Of course not." Esperanza's lips form a smile, but the
emotions seeping from inside her smell more like sadness
than joy.

Cloe flicks her hand in a quick wave, and we finally
head up the gravelly hill away from Esperanza and Nando,
away from Gus and his sheep, and away from the barn.

"I'm taking you to my favorite place in the whole world,
Stella," Cloe says, hitching the delicious-smelling bag higher
on her back.

I stop to do my business under a tree at the back of

the field that has all the play equipment and inhale another gulp of the morning. When I finish, Cloe leads me toward a trail laden with animal scents. The heady perfume of common forest creatures, like deer and rabbit, mixes and mingles with the more exotic aroma of a fox and some sort of large cat that lives off small game—not your average house cat or barn cat, that's for sure.

As my nose leads us deeper into the forest, I sniff for dogs but don't smell any. The air cools as we trek farther into the trees. My tail stands straight as a fence post. Cloe hums as we crest a small hill and then follow the trail down into a little dip. The fresh scent of running water reaches my nose before I hear it or see it. Somehow, I know that's where we're headed.

Unlike the quiet farm behind us, weighted down with heat, the cool forest is alive with bird chatter and the drone of insects. The tinkle of running water greets us when we step into the clearing. My nose twitches. My body trembles. The place is swarming with fascinating smells. Every animal in the forest must drink somewhere along this stream, and apparently a couple of human boys do as well. Beneath the enjoyable scent of so many living things, another aroma prickles my nose—something explosive, gunpowder maybe. Out of habit, my butt smacks the ground. My lower jaw drops. My ears lift, and I whine like Connie taught me.

"What is it, Stella?" Cloe slides the bag off her shoulder,

unzips it, and pulls out a blanket, a crinkly bag filled with meat and cheese, and a book.

Standing, I circle and prepare to alert again.

"What's gotten into you, girl? Huh?" Her eyes search the bank then the dark woods around the clearing. "This is what you were doing at the hardware store the other day, isn't it, silly girl?"

My hackles rise. Something about the scent of gunpowder out here in the forest doesn't smell right. I whimper but hold my position.

"You're okay, Stella. Nothing to worry about here." She waves the blanket on the air like a flag then spreads it on the ground.

I watch as she lowers herself to the blanket. When I don't move, she pats the ground, inviting me to join her. I glance from her face to the forest on the other side of the creek and then back to her face.

"No, Stella. We can't go over there. That's Vern's property. If he caught either of us over there, it would not be good."

Whimpering again, I give the leash a gentle tug. But it's no use. She opens the container of food she brought in her bag, releasing a cloud of meaty goodness. Detecting explosive smells was my job when I worked with Connie, but here with Cloe, other things are important—like *touch*, and *watch me*, and Cloe's chemical smells, and roast beef. Plus, the delicious perfume floating from the bag distracts me from the stink of gunpowder. So I join her on the blanket, resting my hip against her leg. As she feeds me tiny bits of cheese, she flips pages in the book she brought.

When she looks down at me, she smiles. "This is my favorite book, Stella. You're going to love it. It's called *Charlotte's Web*. Charlotte is a spider, and she's so wise. Listen, okay?"

I gaze up at her as she runs her free hand from the top of my head and down my back over and over again. The sun ripples through the leaves like water, warming my fur. My eyes begin to droop while she stares into the book and says long strings of soothing words. My head bobs a little.

"Are you listening, Stella Bella?" Cloe asks. "I love this part. Wilbur says, 'It is not often that someone comes along who is a true friend and good writer.' Isn't that a lovely compliment?"

She reaches into the crinkly paper bag, breaks off a tiny bit of yummy sandwich, and feeds it to me from her hand.

"'It is not often that someone comes along who is a true friend and good writer.' I think I would love it very much if I could be both of those someday, Stella—a good writer and a good friend. I love Mom, and the farm, and my life here. But I'm not going to lie. My seizures make things awkward sometimes, especially with other kids."

I lift my ears to listen, not sure why her voice dropped

so low, or more important, why her hand stopped moving. She sighs and then goes back to looking at her book. The rhythm of her words washes over me, and my eyes grow heavy again. A light breeze tickles my whiskers—the first breeze I've felt in days, maybe the first breeze since I arrived on the farm. And it carries a hint of rain, and rabbits, and the two boys I smelled over by the creek.

My head tilts at the crack of a twig in the distance, but Cloe doesn't seem to hear it. She's lost in her book. My nose wiggles, left then right. I lift one ear then the other. The boys are heading this way, bringing with them the stink of gunpowder and the faint aroma of . . . blood.

I stand and whine. This is not good.

"Are you bored, Stella?" Cloe asks. "Are you ready to go home?"

I know that word—*home*. Yes, I want to go home, where it's safe. Lifting both ears, I growl low and soft at the sound of the approaching boys. But Cloe still doesn't hear them.

"Maybe you'd like *Because of Winn-Dixie* better," she says digging around in her bag. She freezes when she finally hears something—the sound of feet crunching through the thick leaves on the forest floor.

"Who is—" She scrambles to her feet.

The hair on my back stands up. The boys' clothes are painted with the smell of gunpowder and the blood of a young squirrel. I'm not wild about squirrels. They're not much different than mice or rats. I enjoy barking at them and even running them up trees, but I would never draw blood. But these boys have done something to draw blood.

Opening my mouth, I yawn nervously, wanting to get Cloe back to the farm and Esperanza. But it's too late, the boys enter the clearing—one tall and lean, the other short and wide.

"Look what we've got here, Beau. A trespasser on Uncle Vern's land." The taller of the two lifts a gun to his shoulder, clicks its handle, and looks down the length of the thing toward Cloe. He closes one eye.

The other boy laughs but doesn't smile. He smells aggressive.

I growl, warning them not to come any closer to my girl.

"Oh! It's a vicious attack beagle. I'm terrified." The short one lifts his hands to his mouth, his eyes wide.

"You should be," Cloe says, standing up. "If I tell your uncle you pointed a gun at me, you'll be grounded for life."

"You're trespassing," the tall one says, lowering the gun and sneering. "Plus it's just a BB gun."

"Actually, you're the one trespassing. Your Uncle Vern's property starts on the other side of the creek." She plants a small hand on her hip. "Ask your uncle if you don't believe me."

"Maybe we will," the tall one says, but his voice has lost its confidence.

The smaller one brushes his boot back and forth through the leaves under his feet—back and forth. The breeze lifts a sweaty piece of hair off his forehead, and he glares into my eyes. "Or maybe we won't."

Cloe bends down. Yanking her blanket off the ground, she rolls it in a ball and crams it into her bag.

"Leaving so soon?" the tall boy asks.

"Yeah, I just noticed this part of the forest kind of stinks." Slinging the bag over her shoulder, she pats her leg, signaling me to stay close.

"Is that supposed to be an insult?" He steps forward.

"Take it however you like. I'm just saying something is starting to smell rotten, so I'm leaving." Cloe turns her back on the boys and marches toward the trail leading back to the farm. "Let's go, Stella," she says.

I follow, glancing back over my shoulder. I realize that she's left the book she loves in the grass near the creek. But she doesn't stop moving away from the boys and away from her book.

"Come on, Beau. There's squirrels begging to be got rid of all over these woods." The tall boy clicks the handle on his gun again.

Cloe marches forward, her jaw firm. I trot alongside her, thankful for the smell of rain brewing in the air and for the growing distance between my girl and those horrid boys with their harsh voices and their harsh smells.

Chapter Thirteen

Despite the thunder and the upturned leaves last week, the sky refuses to release a single drop of rain. The ground around the farm is as dry as a bone baking in the sun—so dry it cracks in places, opening up tiny, jagged crevices in the earth. The cracks scratch the pads of my paws, so I stick to grassy areas when I'm not in the barn, or sitting on the front porch with Cloe, or riding somewhere in the car.

Each day the temperature continues to rise. The only time it's cool enough to play outdoor games on the equipment behind the barn is either early in the morning or late in the evening after the sun drops behind the towering hills.

This afternoon, Cloe and I sit on a blanket in the shade beside the house. My eyes grow heavy in the heat as she reads aloud from a book. I recognize many of the words—*farmer, dog, squirrel*. Cloe rubs circles on the tips of my ears with her free hand then pauses. This is a fine story, but Cloe doesn't read with the same enthusiasm that she did with the other book down at the creek. She seems to have forgotten where she left it. Glancing up at her face, I wish I had real words, so I could tell her.

"You're bored, aren't you, girl?" she asks.

My ears perk up at her tone. Tilting my head, I stare into her eyes. We've played so many games for so many days that I'm learning to do more than just trust her. I'm learning to read her mind by studying her facial expressions, the sound of her breathing, even the frequency of her blinking. Soon, I'll know her as well as I knew Connie.

Yesterday, when we played in the sandy field up the hill from the barn, I placed my front feet on the teeter object that makes the terrible sounds when it pivots from one position to another because I knew that's what Cloe wanted me to do. When my first paw grazed the board, she gave me several bits of hot dog. When I inched forward and bravely planted my other front paw on the board, she emptied her entire treat pouch right there in front of me. I devoured handfuls of hot dog, bologna, and cheese, standing there with two paws on the board and two paws on the warm sand.

For some reason, it's very important to her that I master that game, but I can't see the point. I trust her completely, but I don't know if I can trust such a noisy contraption—or why I should even try.

Nuzzling her hand, I rest my head on my paws and watch her face, waiting to see if she's going to continue with this story or if it's time to check on Esperanza or play a game.

"You want me to keep reading?"

Whimpering, I nudge her hand again. She laughs and starts into another long, ropey strand of words. She reads, turns a page, reads, then turns another. Eventually, my heavy eyelids win, and I drift in and out of a light sleep. When the world around me goes oddly silent, I snap to attention.

Cloe has stopped reading. "What?" she asks, laughing. "I had to stop. You were snoring so loud I couldn't concentrate."

Standing, I yawn and hunch my spine toward the sky like Oscar does. The sun hangs just above the tip of the hills. Very soon, the tallest trees will block some of the light and heat, and we'll get a tiny bit of relief.

"You want to play, Stella Bella?" Cloe asks.

Yes! Yes! I want to play.

After a quick trip to the feed room, we head up the hill to what I've decided is a doggy playground. The rich smell of liver and fish flows from the pouch secured at Cloe's waist. I bounce a little, completely unfazed by the hot, dry earth beneath my paws.

We warm up with a quick game of *watch me* and *touch* then proceed to the jumps Cloe has added to our playtime. She practically beams with light every time I launch myself over one of the silly little red-and-yellow rails. Though I must admit, it feels nice to sail through the air with my feet tucked tightly under my chest—briefly free of the weight of the world.

"Good, girl!" Cloe shouts when I go out in the direction of her pointed finger and jump a series of three jumps then race back to her to sit and wait for a treat.

My tail wags as I inhale the treat and bounce around her feet, waiting for the next command. "Walk it," she says, pointing to a ramp that leads up to a long, narrow board then ends in another ramp that descends to the sand.

We've been practicing this game for a while now too. The first time we did it, Cloe lined the dog walk with tiny bits of bologna. I snuffled up a piece, then stepped to the next and the next. Before I knew it, I'd eaten my way up and over the entire obstacle. At the canine facility with Connie, I worked on a similar piece of equipment, so it really isn't that great of an accomplishment. But I love how Cloe claps her hands, like she thinks I'm the smartest, bravest dog in the world. And I like the view from up here on the dog walk and the scent clouds floating in the air.

From up here, I have a better view of the surrounding trees and their inverted leaves. I hope those upturned leaves mean what I think they do—rain. Nando and the sheep and Esperanza could all use it.

"Come on, girl." Cloe claps her hands, and I dart toward her, forgetting the leaves and everything else. "You're a superstar. All you've got left to do is the teeter. Then we'll be ready to show you off to Mama."

I sit, tilting my head for a better view of her face.

"You want to try it again?" She wiggles a tiny piece of liver back and forth above my head. "Are you ready?"

Yes, yes. If she's asking if I want that piece of liver, my answer is yes.

She steps toward the noisy contraption I avoid whenever I can. I follow, carefully placing one paw on the board. The teeter doesn't thump or bang.

"Good, girl," she says, waving the bit of meat in front of my quivering nose, then moving it away from me.

Not thrilled by her request to follow, I lift a second paw and place it on the board. I peer up at her, waiting to be rewarded with handfuls of meat or cheese, but all I get is the tiny piece of liver in her hand.

"You've got to go farther today," she says, pulling out a larger hunk of liver and placing it a few inches higher on the board.

Stretching my neck as far as I can, I reach for the meat

with no luck. Digging down deep, I try to be brave and stretch just a little farther. I've extended my head and neck so far that my belly practically scrapes the board. Hoping to pull the meat forward with my tongue, I lick the board repeatedly.

"Come on, girl. You can do it," Cloe says.

My mouth watering, I stare at the meat then at Cloe, begging her to help me.

"You can do it, girl," she says again.

I inch forward. The pads of my back paws rest half on the board, half on the sand.

"Yes! Good girl, Stella! You can do it. Come on." Her hands flap together in light applause.

I move forward a couple of inches, then a couple more. Afraid to look back, I focus my eyes straight ahead on the hunk of meat and creep forward. When I finally reach it, I swallow it in one bite. Then I freeze. With all four paws on the board, I'm quite some distance off the ground and don't know how to back down. I crouch, hoping to hold the board steady. The last thing I want is for it to move, or worse, make a booming sound like the explosion I remember from my last time in the airport.

I start to pant. My pads moisten with sweat. My ears droop. I just want down.

Off.

Away.

Cloe takes one step back, toward the other end of the board. She reaches with her arms above her head. "I'm going to lift it just an inch or two," she says, her voice low and soothing. Bending her knees, she pulls down on the opposite end of the board that had been pointing to the sky.

When the thing moves, I glance back and forth, back and forth, trying to decide which way to jump, anticipating the ear-shattering, earthshaking sound the teeter is going to make if she pulls any harder.

Rocking back on my rear end, I collapse into a full crouch with my stomach stuck to the board like one of Connie's Velcro belts.

As I tense my hindquarters and prepare to jump, Cloe steps toward me and places one firm hand on my back and the other on my belly. I whine, and she plucks me from the board, placing me gently on the ground.

"You're getting there. Good girl!" she says, tousling my ears. "I think that's enough for today. Want to go to the creek? Mom said Vern's nephews finally went home."

I wag my tail, thankful to have all four paws on the ground once again.

"Let's go." She waves my leash in one hand and pats her thigh with the other.

I follow, thrilled to have an opportunity to prove myself off leash. She and Esperanza have been doing this more often, allowing me a few minutes to roam freely, as long as I stay close by. If I get too distracted by the scent of a squirrel or rabbit and wander too far, they call me back and clip my leash to my collar. Today, I'm determined to please Cloe and stick right to her side no matter what furry little creatures tempt me with their smells.

"You deserve a quick walk after that," she says.

I trot alongside. As we cross the line of shadows into the forest, the temperature drops. It crosses my mind that we didn't tell Esperanza where we're going. But Cloe's chemicals smell good today. She hasn't had an episode since that day she fell down in the hot parking lot. My nose hasn't twitched with concern in many days. And it's almost dinnertime, so I know she doesn't plan to stay gone long.

Plus, it just feels so good in the shade. Cloe's feet *shush* the fallen pine needles. The afternoon is pretty close to perfect, except for the lack of rain. I bounce along as we follow the familiar path to the stream, happy Cloe will finally find the book she lost.

When we start downhill, I smell fresh water and something else—something that reminds me of the boys with the gun and the squirrel blood. I freeze.

"You're okay, Stella," Cloe says. "We're almost there."

When I don't move, she bends down, clips the leash to my collar, and pulls me forward. I dig in my paws, determined to turn back. She tugs a little harder. Even though she's just a young girl, she's outweighs me by a lot. I whimper, but it's no use. A dog must follow her girl, and I do. But my drooping ears tell it all.

A minute later, the rush of water reaches our ears. Then we're in the clearing. Glancing back the way we came, I pant. The muscles in my hind legs and along my back twitch, eager to sit and alert like I've been trained to do. But Cloe and Esperanza are never interested in my alerting signals.

"You need some water," she says, tugging me toward the stream before my behind can smack the ground.

So I slink forward until she stops in her tracks.

"What in the—" She stares, openmouthed, at ripped papers scattered on the ground.

A breeze picks up, tickling my whiskers, bringing with it smells from the opposite direction. My tail stands straight and stiff, the hair on my back bristling. The boys are here somewhere with a new smell—smoke and acid. They've been burning something. I sit, no longer able to control the urge to alert.

"Come on, girl. Why are you always doing that? Are you trying to tell me something?"

Finally, finally, someone seems to be paying attention to my most important signal.

As Cloe bends to pick up a handful of scraps, my tail wags weakly. Then her head swivels around the clearing, and she gasps. "My book. *Charlotte's Web*. It's ruined. Stella, who could have—"

She straightens and peers into the forest. A whiff of anxiety leaks from behind her bare knees and beneath her arms. Leaves rustle and whisper around us. A tree limb creaks, unused to the movement of air. The first crack of thunder rumbles in the distance. I tug in the direction of the farm. We're finally in for a storm, and that seems to me like the perfect reason to head straight for home.

I bark. When I do, the forest around us explodes. The air sizzles and pops with the staccato *crack crack crack* of countless tiny explosions. My head snaps back and forth.

I turn to run. Cloe turns with me, and we freeze. The boys block our retreat.

Glaring at us, the taller of the two flicks his thumb on a fist-sized device. When he does, a small flame jumps from an opening at the top.

"Happy Fourth of July," the blocky one—Beau—sneers, holding a cylinder of paper up toward the flame.

"I thought you went home." Cloe inches closer to me.

"Surprise." The tall boy peers down his nose at us.

"Stop!" Cloe waves him off with her hand, dropping my leash in the process. "Put the lighter away. There's a forest fire warning. Besides, we're leaving."

"Bwack, bwack, bwaaack," the tall one says, sounding like a sick chicken.

Beau dangles the thread hanging from the paper cylinder over the flame until it sparks to life with a light of its own. A growl forms low in my neck. I try to move toward him, but my slick pads slip on the carpet of pine needles.

Then he lifts his arm, winding up to throw.

As the burning cylinder rockets toward us, Cloe lets out a bloodcurdling scream.

Chapter Fourteen

Time seems to slow. Every muscle in my body tenses, and my heart jerks to a stop inside my chest. When the burning packet smacks the ground near my front paws, it hisses and spits angry sparks against my belly. I freeze, willing myself to stand firm, to stand with my girl, despite the biting heat on my sensitive skin and the desperate urge to run for my life.

"Look out, Stella!" Cloe swats at the thing with her tennis shoe, trying to kick it away from me.

I try to bark at Beau, but all I manage is a half-hearted whine. His small eyes remain locked on the burning packet. He's transfixed like a Jack Russell terrier with a tennis ball.

Beside him, the tall boy lights a second packet, shouts something I don't understand, then launches it in our direction as well. My heart jerks back to life, banging hard against my ribs. My eyes dart around the clearing, looking for an escape. My head says to stay with my girl, but a deeper, wilder part of me panics, warning me to run.

"Take cover," Beau yells. As he bolts for the trees, more small, colorful, paper-wrapped packages spill to the ground around his feet.

"Stella, come," Cloe says, her voice calm and authoritative as she steps backward toward the creek.

Cocking my head in her direction, I whimper. I love her so much. It should be simple—stay with my girl. Good dogs are loyal. They stand with their handlers in spite of danger, even in spite of death.

There was a time when I was a good dog. I identified many dangerous objects and chemicals and prevented them from getting onto airplanes. I did good, important work. But one mistake resulted in Connie's death. And no amount of good work will ever make up for that.

Ever.

I failed Connie the day of the explosion in the airport. It was the day before Thanksgiving, the busiest day of the year. Connie and I had worked much longer than usual, and I was tired and thinking about dinner and the turkey at home in the oven. At about the same time that I caught a whiff of something explosive, a security man at the airport opened a large glass door to start another line so travelers could move through security more quickly.

When he did, the airflow in the room shifted, causing an unexpected cross-breeze. The sudden movement of air confused me for a second, and that was all it took—one second—for a bad man to set off an explosion that blasted upward. Suitcases, children, and dogs near the ground were okay, but taller adults like Connie weren't.

"Stella, come," Cloe shouts again, her face as white as one of the blankets on her bed.

When I glance in her direction, the packet closest to my belly explodes, ripping through my skin. My ears ring. Smoke burns my nose.

And I bolt.

Images from the airport flash in my head: the lifeless form of an old man with a cane, Alexa—my favorite security employee—clutching her head, and Connie lying on the white floor, her brown hair fanned out around her face like a sunburst.

I fly through the forest, sailing over a fallen tree without pausing. My leash catches on a limb, whiplashing my neck painfully before I am able to tug it free. I bite my tongue and run harder, faster. The pads of my paws burn. My lungs sting. My heart threatens to burst from my chest as I continue to race for my life.

The trees blur and blend around me, like ominous clouds of brown and black. A thicket of briars bites and tears at my face, lips, ears, but I press on. When I shoot out of the far side of the brambles, I meet a rushing creek head-on. Unable to stop, I rock back on my hind legs in an exhausted attempt to heave myself up and over the running water.

But my tired legs fail me, and I belly flop on a slick rock halfway across the creek. The frigid water does for me what I couldn't do for myself. It swipes the violent memories of the explosion in the airport out of my head, clearing my vision like windshield wipers on a car.

Hanging my head, I slide off the rock and into the stream. When my nose and mouth sink beneath the water, I'm too weak to fight—too weak to care. My eyes flutter closed. The water rushing around my head drowns out the rest of the world. As my vision fades, an odd whispering sound mixes with the tumble of water.

Holding my breath, I listen.

"You must do the thing you cannot do," a very strong, very familiar voice says over the rushing of the water. It's Connie. Her voice washes over me, soothing the scratches and bruises covering my body from nose to tail.

I whine, hoping she'll come to me, hoping she'll rub the top of my head, scratch behind my ears, run a gentle hand along my neck and back. I want her to make everything better.

"You must do the thing you cannot do," she says again, more firmly this time. Suddenly, I understand those words—the words Connie repeated so often from her favorite book. "You made a mistake, Stella. We all make mistakes. That doesn't make us bad dogs. You can do this. You can do anything. Do the thing you think you cannot do, girl. Do it for me."

The sound of Connie's voice fades. Lifting my head out of the water, I blink, searching for her on the bank of the creek. I want to be with Connie. I want her to stay with me. She's the one who makes me brave and good. The icy water stings my face, and I struggle to my feet, shivering.

Shaking my head, I glance at the darkening forest closing in around the creek. I know what I need to do.

I must do the thing I think I cannot do. I must head back into the heat and the sound of those horrible exploding packets, find my girl, and take her home.

Chapter Fifteen

Lifting my nose, I sniff, trying to locate the direction of the clearing where I abandoned Cloe. But the cool air blowing in from the west confuses my nose, twisting the hot air that's been pressing down on us for weeks into swirling circles.

Crouching on my belly, I tunnel back into the thicket of brambles beside the creek, hoping to find my way back before the wind and the coming rain wash away the scent of my trail for good.

But the swirling air blows the dusty floor of the forest into confusing puffs of air. My heart drums as I backtrack along what I hope is the correct trail. Then the first crack of lightning breaks the sky, and I freeze with my tail tucked between my legs like a frightened puppy.

A roll of thunder shakes the earth, but I force myself

to trot along in what I hope is the right direction. Heavy clouds block the setting sun, making it difficult to see and forcing me to rely mostly on my nose. A fallen tree slows my progress. When I try to leap over the decaying trunk in the dim light, I forget about the leash dragging behind me. It catches on a knotty limb protruding from the trunk, and pulls my neck back over my shoulder.

When I smack the forest floor, the air whooshes from my lungs. Head flat on the pine needles, I pant. The wind isn't swirling any longer. Now, it slices in one direction, pushing the scents dropped by my paws, other forest animals, and even a couple of humans, in the same direction as the racing clouds.

Lightning strikes again, ripping through the sky. The jagged flash has barely faded when thunder rocks the forest. Around me, tall pines bend at odd angles, more like long blades of grass than trees.

I'm tempted to crawl into the dry space beneath the fallen tree, but I don't. I have to get to Cloe, to make sure her chemicals are okay and to make sure those boys didn't hurt her. She'll be worried sick about me.

I force myself to my feet and tug on the leash. But it's no use. The thing is wedged tight. Leaning forward, I growl as if I'm battling a Doberman for a bone and yank with all my might. All I accomplish is additional pain and bruising around my neck.

I can't quit though—not with Connie's words still ringing in my head. If my muscles aren't strong enough to pull the leash free, maybe my teeth are strong enough to chew myself free. My empty stomach groans as I tear into the leash. I rip, shake, and chew but make little progress. Frustrated, I spin, desperate to free myself and get to Cloe.

A limb snaps high in a nearby tree and crashes to the ground. When I jerk away to avoid it falling on me, my collar slips up my neck, toward my ears. And a genius idea hits.

Pulling the leash free isn't going to work. Eating through it will take forever. I'm going to have to try something else, like focusing on my collar instead of the leash.

I turn to face the fallen tree, rock back on my haunches, and shake my head back and forth until the collar reaches the top of my neck and catches at the base of my ears. I'm so close. I can smell freedom—from this collar at least.

A knife of lightning strikes the top of a nearby tree, and I nearly jump out of my skin. When I move, though, the collar jerks over the top of my head and down my snout, plopping onto the ground with a thump and a jingle of tags. The hair on my head and neck stands on end, but it's not from fear or aggression. Energy hums in the air and through my body—the same kind of energy that sizzles in human houses and lamps.

Despite my fear and aching muscles, I run, then lift

my nose to sniff for Cloe and the farm. What I smell are pigs, lots and lots of corn, and several other vegetables I don't recognize. But I can't be certain of the direction of the smells because they swirl toward me in puffs, not the steady stream of human or animal footsteps I'm used to tracking. Lifting my ears, I peer into the forest, listening for signs of Cloe, but I don't hear anything other than the roar of the wind.

The animal-vegetable smells seem to come from the other side of the hill blocking my path. So I steady my quivering legs and creep in that direction. Keeping my head down and nose close to the ground, I struggle against the oncoming wind to the top of the hill.

When I reach the top and look down, a well-lit house catches my eye. The knot in my chest releases slightly. Lights mean humans. Humans mean help. Help for Cloe and Esperanza. Without hesitation, I move toward the glowing house. Rows and rows of corn, tomatoes, and other vegetables swish eerily behind and along one side of the house. Fat, squat creatures huddle together in the corner of a fenced enclosure on the other side of the house. Pigs! Huge pigs. They're as large as small cars, and they huff and chuff miserably from their cramped pen.

Keeping to the shadows, I creep around the perimeter of the yard toward the pigs. Lightning strikes in the distance. The wind seems to be pushing the storm over the mountains and away from us.

When I crouch near the fence, the pigs amble over to investigate, but they're packed so tightly in the stinking enclosure that only two of them can get their snouts to the fence to sniff at me. I inch closer to investigate. The sliding lock on their gate looks like the one on my crate, so I decide to free them.

With a quick push of my nose, the gate creaks open, and a large dog I hadn't noticed downwind jumps to his feet. He barks, deep and loud.

Freezing, I inhale to gather information. He smells harmless enough—more bark than bite. And I can't blame him for the noise. He's chained to a tree, a strange dog is trespassing on his property, and the pigs he's supposed to be guarding are squealing with joy as they trundle past him to the garden behind the house.

I don't have time to celebrate my kind deed. I need to know if someone here can help me find my girl. As I contemplate my options, the front door opens, spilling bright light onto the porch. Heavy boots clomp forward, and an enormous man steps outside. The wind carries his smell— old meat and gunpowder—my way. It's the man from the store with all the tools, the man who made Esperanza and Cloe uncomfortable.

"Who's there?" He holds a gun at his side. It's much

larger than the one the boys aimed at Cloe earlier. His head jerks in the direction of grunting sounds coming from the corn. "What in the—?"

Rows of corn fall to the ground as if invisible tractors are plowing them down. Delighted snuffling sounds punctuate the snapping of stalks and cracking of raw corncobs.

The man practically growls as he shakes a fist at the sky. "Whoever you are, you're gonna pay!"

The pigs freeze. The dog stiffens.

I don't move. The hair on my back stands at attention. My jaws click closed.

With my heart in my throat, I watch as he lifts his enormous gun to his shoulder and turns toward me. Afraid to move but desperate to run, I crouch low to the ground, trying to make myself invisible.

The man descends a step, the boards creaking beneath his heavy weight.

Taking a deep breath, I prepare to run, but before my paws can propel me into motion, tires crunch on the gravel drive. The man turns his head toward the approaching car. When it turns a bend in the driveway, he lowers his gun. The car has words on the side and unlit lights on the top. It slides to a stop. Then the driver's door opens, and a woman climbs out.

"Evening, Vern," the woman says as she steps around her car and toward him.

"Evening, Deputy. How can I help you?" He nods and props the wide end of the gun on the ground, leaning on it for support.

She gestures toward her car. "I brought your nephews home. Found 'em out on the main road. Mrs. Smart complained about them throwing firecrackers at her mailbox. I'm not sure if you know, Vern, but mailboxes are considered federal property. If they'd actually hit the thing, you'd be facing a big fine. And fireworks are no laughing matter these days. The woods around here are dry as tinder."

I don't need to look at the boys or Vern to recognize their fear. The smell of it hangs heavy in the air even from this distance.

The large man huffs toward her, his jaw set. "Don't worry, Deputy. You won't have a problem with those boys ever again. They'll be apologizing to Mrs. Smart in the morning and picking up litter in the woods sunup to sundown tomorrow."

I don't stick around for the rest of their conversation. I use the distraction to my advantage and run while I have the chance.

And run.

And run.

I do not want anything to do with those boys, that man, or his big gun ever again.

Chapter Sixteen

I run like all our lives—mine, Cloe's, Connie's—depend on it.

And maybe they do.

My eyes sting from the dry heat that still lingers after the storm brushed past. The pads of my feet burn. My lungs threaten to explode. When I don't think I can go another step, a whiff of something familiar grabs my nose and jerks my head to the side. It's not Cloe or the farm. It's not Nando or the sheep. But it's close.

It's the main road. If I follow it long enough, it will eventually take me home. Cloe is a very smart girl. I have to trust that she made better choices than I did and that she headed straight for home and not farther into the forest.

When I reach the pavement, I keep to the shadowy brush at the side of the road. My tongue hangs from the side of my mouth like a dry rope, and my body cries out for rest, but I trudge on. As the last hint of daylight fades, I spy the familiar driveway in the distance, and my heart lifts. Despite the lightness in my chest, the pads of my feet drag in the dirt. When a whiff of something foreign—something that doesn't belong on the farm—creeps into the passages in my nose, my heart clenches again.

The scent of strange humans wafts toward me.

And there are lots of strange humans.

And no sign of Cloe.

I dig my toenails into the hard-packed driveway and push myself forward, determined to figure out what's going on. Every muscle in my body screams. My eyes, nose, and tongue feel like they're coated in sand. When I round the last bend in the driveway, a wave of my worst fears threatens to knock my feet out from under me.

Clusters of cars block the driveway to the barn in one direction and the house in the other. They're parked at odd angles, like the people stopped and jumped out in a hurry. Lights flash on top of one of the vehicles, and a cluster of men and women with badges all over their clothes stands under the big oak near the pasture.

Shaking my head, I blink to clear my eyes. This cannot be happening. It's like the day at the airport all over again.

My nose twitches, nostrils widening with a will of their own. I smell dogs, too—and not Nando or Gus. These are strange dogs, and they belong to these strange people. They must smell me, too, because two of them stand up tall and proud beside their handlers as I approach. They look down their long, pointed noses at me.

I know the type. They're working dogs like me, except they're bigger and tougher-looking and like to throw their muscle around. But they don't scare me. And just to prove it, I stop, stiffen my tail, and whip it back and forth without breaking eye contact with the other dog. Then I lift my nose to the sky and let loose a howl from deep down inside of me.

One of the dogs growls. The human talking halts abruptly.

Taking a couple of steps forward, I inhale and prepare to let loose with another earthshaking yowl.

"Easy, Rex," a man says as he lays a hand on the top of his dog's head. He has a short stick hanging near his waist.

When I open my mouth again, I feel like all the feelings I've been holding in since that day at the airport are blasting out of my throat with the force of my own dangerous explosion.

The strange humans stare at me as if I've grown a second head.

"Oh, thank heavens, Stella, you're home!"

My head whips in the direction of Esperanza's voice. She steps around a blocky woman. One final surge of energy propels me toward her. I half jump, half fling myself in her direction. Nando trots forward, greeting me with a bark and an energetic tail wag as Esperanza pulls me into her arms and showers kisses all over my head and face.

Nuzzling her neck, I sniff for any sign of Cloe. There are scents, but they're old—too old. I whine.

"Where in the world have you been, girl?" Esperanza's strong voice cracks when she speaks. "Where's Cloe?"

I yip at the sound of Cloe's name. My breath comes faster. My sides heave as I pant.

Esperanza tugs on the loose skin at the back of my neck the way Mama did when I was a pup. "She came from the main road. Do you think we should search in that direction first?"

The largest man in the group shakes his head. "No. We should trust the dogs."

"But they're signaling two different directions," Esperanza says. She grips me so tight I can hardly breathe.

"Then we'll split into two groups. But we're not heading out in a third direction on a whim. And we're not wasting any more time talking. Time is of the essence with lost kids—especially lost kids with medical conditions." The man's voice is low and confident, but it does nothing to stop the waves of fear rising from Esperanza's skin or the sweat forming under her arms.

"I'm going with you," Esperanza says.

"I'm not sure—"

"I'm going with you," Esperanza says a second time, looking the man directly in the eyes without any sign of backing down. "Just let me put my dogs away first."

"I don't think it's a good idea. But I'm not going to waste time arguing." He turns his back to us and speaks to the others. "You three take Rex and follow the trail he recognized behind the pasture. I'll take Hunter and start near the house where he signaled."

Esperanza holds me tight against her chest as she scurries toward the barn. I try to squirm free. We should not be heading to the barn. I need to take Esperanza to the creek to find Cloe. That's where she will have gone looking for me. And it's getting darker by the second.

Licking my lips, I try to control my panting. But it's useless. I can't stop thinking of those horrid boys and what they might be doing in the forest. When I see where we're headed, I stop breathing completely. My vision blurs.

No. No. No.

I squirm harder, trying to break free. My toenails dig into Esperanza's arm, and she winces.

"Stella, be good, girl. Settle down. I have to go find Cloe."

I understand those words—*find Cloe*.

Yes, *find Cloe*. I need to find Cloe too.

But Esperanza shoves me in the crate in the feed room

and locks the door. I bark and spin, bark and spin, bark and spin as she turns her back and leaves Nando and me behind.

I claw at the hard floor and bite the wires.

I'm trapped.

Stuck.

Cut off from my girl.

Rocking back on my haunches, I tilt my head to the sky and wail, begging them to come back for me. Nando paces back and forth near the crate. But the humans don't listen.

They. Do. Not. Listen.

When their loud voices and the barking of their dogs fades away from the barn, I rattle the crate and cry. I won't stop either. I'll rattle and cry until my toenails fall off and my throat tears apart, or both. I have to free myself and find my girl.

There are no other options.

Chapter Seventeen

I don't know how much time passes before Oscar slinks into the feed room and sidles up beside my crate. All I know is that I have to get to Cloe, so I fling myself against the wires, hoping Oscar will do something—anything—to help.

Instead, he narrows his eyes and hisses.

So I fling myself against the wires a second time. When I do, his claws snap out like a whip, and he catches the sensitive skin flap near my mouth, shredding my already sore lip. Whining, I retreat to the back of the crate to lick my wounds.

Suddenly, it dawns on me that Esperanza was so upset she forgot to secure the gate with the hooked cord. Despite my injuries, I want to slather Oscar in kisses. His swat was exactly what I needed to interrupt my panic and help me think more clearly. Now that I'm focused, I know exactly what I need to do—work the latch free.

And in no time, that's exactly what I do. Much to Nando and Oscar's dismay, I bolt past them and out of the feed room before the door swings all the way open. When my paws hit the concrete aisle of the barn, I break into a full gallop and race through the small opening in the sliding barn door.

Then I'm free, free, free and racing across the crispy grass to the playfield behind the barn. Esperanza and the clumps of people with their important dogs are gone. The farm is eerily quiet, like it's waiting for something big to happen.

Nando glides along behind me, head and tail below his shoulders, focused. But he doesn't try to herd me back to the barn. For once, he lets me do my thing without trying to protect or control me. It's almost as if he senses my new-found determination. As we pass the pasture, Gus takes a few steps away from his sheep to follow our progress along the fence. His tail swishes back and forth in a slow wag, as if he's rooting for me as well.

Oddly, the dogs with the long, pointy noses seem to have led their handlers away from the trail to the creek. Tracking dogs don't make mistakes often. But the entire farm is full of Cloe's smell, and all the wind this afternoon has made the pockets and paths of Cloe's scent fuzzy at the edges.

To further complicate matters, a faint whiff of smoke hangs on the breeze. The tracking dogs will realize their mistake soon and either backtrack in this direction or change tracks entirely. But I don't have time to wait for them. Cloe is my girl, and I don't want her to be frightened by strange, barking dogs. I want to find her and bring her home myself.

I press my nose to the ground and follow her odor toward the creek. His head hanging low, Nando pads along behind me on the forest trail. The tracks Cloe and I left earlier are definitely the freshest, which means she never doubled back to the barn. If I know my girl, she headed further into the forest to look for me—to try to save me. Thankful for my nose and the last remaining bit of light in the sky, I climb the big hill that leads into the clearing near the creek. The sharp bite of smoke in the air intensifies. My moist paws slip on the hard ground.

Those horrible boys with their crackling packets, sparking flames, and guilty faces are to blame. I just know it. And from where I stand, it smells like they've set the whole forest on fire.

When Nando barks, I glance over my shoulder. He stands frozen in his tracks, ears lifted, head rotating back and forth as he tries to zero in on a popping and crackling in the distance. A gust of dry air invades my eyes, nose, and gaping mouth. I drop my head lower to the ground in search of fresh air. Despite the blistering heat and biting smoke, Cloe's scent clearly covers the undisturbed pine needles on the forest floor.

I'd recognize her smell even with a bag full of meat and cheese next to my head.

It's Cloe, and her scent trail leads directly into the highest concentration of heat and smoke. The breathable air beneath the smoke all but disappears. My chest tightens as I peer down the hill into the smoldering trees. If Cloe has fallen down again because of her chemicals, if she's overcome by smoke, I'm not sure I'll be able to save her. Worse, I'm not sure anyone else will have time to save her either.

I whine and charge down the hill toward the clearing and my girl.

Chapter Eighteen

Nose to the ground, I race around the clearing, then up and down the creek bank. Cloe's tracks are everywhere, but there is no sign of her. Nando wades into the water, sniffing the stones that protrude as I double back to the edge of the clearing where we had the standoff with the horrible boys.

An unbearable curtain of heat drapes this part of the forest. The wind blows the remaining bits of the boy's burned paper packages around. I smell charcoal and sulfur. My eyes widen at the mound of unignited colorful packets lying at the base of a tree, tempting the fire to move in and ignite them as well.

I have to find Cloe, so I scan the area again, this time concentrating on using my eyes and nose together. What I spot this time is much worse than smoke or piles of flammable packets of paper—it's actual fire.

The flames are not huge, but they're hungry. And they're growing as they lick at the brittle twigs and leaves carpeting the forest floor. And they're moving this way.

Barking, I race back to Nando. He lifts his head to return my bark. Together, we bound into the forest on the opposite side of the creek. I'm tempted to run headlong into the forest, but I know deep down that I need to use my nose. I need to trust it. I need to trust myself.

We all make mistakes. That's what Connie said. I made one mistake—one time—long ago that day in the airport. But that mistake doesn't define me. It doesn't erase all the good work I've done. And it won't stop me from doing the most important work of my life taking place right here, right now in this forest.

Despite the smoke, despite the flames, despite the fear gripping my chest, I pause to evaluate the situation. I need to let my nose do what it does best. So I lower my head to the ground, block out the sound of the advancing fire, and complete a few zigs and zags across the ground on this side of the creek. On my third pass, the aroma of cookies and vinegar ignites my nostrils.

Cloe!

I've got her.

She did head deeper into the forest in search of me.

I bark, signaling for Nando to follow. The underbrush thickens as we head farther into the forest. The staccato *ack ack ack* of explosives breaks in the clearing far behind us. I jump. The fire must have found the abandoned mound of explosives. It will grow now with even more fuel to feed it.

My heart clenches in my chest, and I lose Cloe's scent for just a second. I lose my footing, too, and stumble nose-first to the ground. I've never bitten anyone in my life, but if I could get my teeth on those horrid boys who dropped those horrid packets in the clearing, I might just clamp onto an ankle or a wrist and never let go.

Vision blurred by heat and smoke, Nando trips over me and tumbles to the ground as well.

Refusing to be distracted by anything or anyone, I shake my head and leap to my feet. The explosions have ended. But a light wind blows at our backs, carrying the heat and smoke toward us, which means the hungry fire isn't far behind. Nando and I don't have much time.

I drop my nose to the ground and sniff. Without pausing, we follow my nose deeper and deeper into the forest. Cloe's scent grows stronger. We're practically on top of her. I can *feel* her as much as I can smell her. I lift my head to survey the surrounding woods. A massive fallen tree blocks my view. Cloe must be just on the other side of the trunk. I bark to let her know I'm coming. Bounding ahead of me and vaulting over the tree like a deer, Nando barks

too. I'm not as graceful, but I'm determined and not far behind. Landing with a thump, I scramble to my feet on the
other side.

What I see stops me in my tracks.

It's Cloe, but she lies in a tangled heap on the forest
floor—unmoving and unresponsive—despite the fact that
Nando is licking her face.

Chapter Nineteen

No. No. No.

This cannot be happening—not to my girl. Not again.

Cloe lies frozen in time and space, her wavy, dark hair fanned out around her head, just like Connie's was that day in the airport.

I race to her, covering her face and neck and the corners of her mouth in kisses, begging her to wake up. But she doesn't move. I nuzzle her hand, snuffle her ears, huff into her hair.

Nothing.

But there is hope. Her chemical smell is overwhelming, but it's still *her* chemical smell. It is not the outside-of-a-human smell. It is not the smell of the shell of a human. She's still in there somewhere. And I'm going to get her out. And Nando is going to help.

I bark at him, loud and sharp, then grab Cloe by the collar of her shirt and pull. But she doesn't move and neither does Nando. I bark again. He whines. I yank on her shirt again, trying to show him what we need to do. We need to drag Cloe away from the fire to safety. But the dog who can chase sheep with the energy of a swarm of grasshoppers just stands there, staring at me.

Releasing Cloe, I step behind Nando, nip at his heels, and growl. When I have his attention, I return to Cloe, sit on my haunches and pull on her shirt with all my might. She barely moves. But Nando steps forward tentatively.

I tilt my head back and bark from low in my chest. I sound more like a Doberman pinscher than a beagle. If I didn't know myself, I'd be frightened. Thankfully, Nando moves to join me and tug at Cloe's shirt. With his help, we make a little progress. But not enough.

We pant. My sweaty paws slip on the slick pine needles. The heat and crackle of the fire presses toward us in waves. We'll be overtaken, consumed in a few minutes.

But I will not give up. I bark and growl and yank at Cloe's clothing.

And she stirs.

She stirs.

I lick her face. *I'm here. I'm here.*

I would give anything to speak all the human words trapped in my head. But I can't, so I raise my head and bark. I bark to the sky. To Connie. To Esperanza. I bark. And bark. And bark.

And I don't stop until I think I might faint from exhaustion. As I'm licking Cloe's hand and mustering my strength for another round of barking, a new sound catches my attention. My head whips toward Nando, lying nervously at Cloe's feet. He jumps to his feet. He hears it, too.

It's not packages of paper exploding.

It's not the crack or pop of advancing flames.

It's not the wind.

It's dogs! Several of them. And they're coming this way. And they have humans with them.

I sit at attention, rest one paw on Cloe's chest, then fling my head back, and bark—loud and deep and low.

Even the sound of my barking cannot drown out the crashing noise of dogs and humans hurdling toward us. When the familiar smells of sheep and soap and corn reach my nose, my heart blossoms with hope. It's Esperanza.

"I'm coming, Stella! I'm coming!" she screams.

I spin in one quick circle, barely able to control myself but not willing to leave my girl. I sit back on the ground, bark, and wait.

After what seems like forever, Esperanza breaks through the brush in the distance. She's followed closely by several of the strange humans from the farm and the big dog named Rex. Tears stream down her face, leaving tracks on her sooty cheeks. She stumbles over a tree root, catches herself, and gallops forward.

"Good girl, Stella! Good girl," she says as she collapses to her knees beside Cloe.

I whine but remain firmly planted on my behind, just the way Connie trained me to do for *find-it-and-alert*. Nando nuzzles Esperanza's arm.

"Yes, Nando. You're a good boy, too," she says as she lowers her face to Cloe's. With one hand gently under Cloe's neck, she uses the other to squeeze Cloe's wrist. She glances over her shoulder at the large man with the dog. "Her pulse is strong, but we need to get her out of here. She has epilepsy."

The man nods as he speaks into a large black phone. "We've got her but need medical personnel, ASAP."

I nuzzle Cloe's neck as Esperanza examines her face and arms, but I remain seated like a good dog.

"Can I lift her?" one of the big men asks. "We'll save time if we head to the road."

"Yes, that should be fine." Esperanza kisses Cloe's face then pulls Nando and me in for a hug.

"Those are pretty impressive dogs you've got there," a woman in a hat says.

"Yes. Yes, they are." Esperanza pats her thigh, signaling for Nando and me to stay close to her.

"Especially the little one." The woman bends down to

run a hand along my back as I pass. "Is she a seizure alert dog?"

"No. She's—" Esperanza turns to look at me. When she does, her eyes look inside of me.

The woman shrugs. "The way she was sitting there— something about the set of her jaw reminded me of a Labrador retriever I saw doing that once." Straightening, she moves to assist her fellow officers.

I hold Esperanza's gaze. It's like we're talking without words, like she really, truly understands what I'm thinking and what I would say to her if I had words.

Despite my torn lip and aching muscles, despite my worry over Cloe, I smile up at her.

One of the large men lifts Cloe gently from the ground. Nando, Esperanza, and I follow close behind. No one speaks except for the large man with the phone. I understand bits and pieces of what he says—*fire, forest, hurry.*

A few minutes later, we're met by more people who place Cloe on a hard board. I spin and whine as a strange woman loops slippery, collarless leashes around my neck and Nando's. We follow these new people out to the main road and to a parked ambulance with flashing lights.

Esperanza squats down to face us. "You two are heroes. I'll take care of Cloe from here. I promise. You go home and take care of the farm. I'll be there as soon as I can."

When she turns away from us, I whine. I do not want

to be separated from her or Cloe. The last time someone I loved left in an ambulance, I never saw her again. Tugging at the leash, I try to follow. But it's no use. With the leash tightening around my neck, I can't even whine.

Chapter Twenty

Back at the farm, Nando and I pace back and forth in the feed room where one of the kind strangers left us. Even this far from the creek and locked inside the barn, I can still smell the biting scent of smoke on the air.

When I think I can't possibly patrol the feed room one more time, a large truck with wailing sirens breaks the silence and slides to a stop near the barn. A group of men, dragging what sounds like heavy equipment, tromp up the hill and toward the woods. Nando and I bark, but no one comes to release us.

Listening carefully, I track the sound of their footsteps as they travel deeper into the forest. When I can't hear them any longer, I turn to my nose for information. My sides ache with the effort. But as the night wears on, the sharp smell of the smoke fades. When I'm sure the fire is out, I allow myself to lie down beside Nando in front of the door and wait for Esperanza.

Despite my concern for Cloe and the empty feeling inside my chest, my eyes grow heavy. At some point, I wake to the sound of the men loading their truck and leaving.

My body aches and my stomach growls, but the blistering temperature seems to have cooled a few degrees. As the moon rises farther in the sky, Nando and I drift in and out of restless sleep. When the heavy barn door finally rumbles open, Nando and I scramble to our feet. I smell Esperanza before I hear her footsteps or see her face. Beneath her usual sheep-soap-corn-perfume are fresh medical odors that remind me of Doc Collins. Cloe's scents are there, too, but hidden even further below the others.

"Hey, guys!" Esperanza squats down to greet us at eye level.

Nando covers her face in kisses while I huff and sniff her shoes and pant legs for information about Cloe.

"You did really good work," she says as she squishes Nando's face against hers with one hand. She runs the other gently down the length of my back. I might purr like Oscar if I weren't so worried about Cloe. Instead, I whine, prodding her for information.

"Let's eat, guys. Then I'll take you to see Cloe." She walks to the big cabinet, her footsteps slow and tired on the floor.

Yes! Cloe!

She grabs our bowls, dumps more kibble than usual into each of them, then sets them on the ground. I nudge the dry food around with my nose and glance at Nando. For once, he devours his food faster than I do. I swallow a couple of bites then stare up at Esperanza.

"Not hungry, girl?" she asks.

I whine.

"I think I know what will make you feel better. Come on," she says.

Nando and I follow her toward the house, pausing only long enough for the world's fastest potty break. As we approach the empty car parked in front of the house, the most wonderfully glorious fragrance in the history of the universe tickles my nose and fills my nostrils.

Cloe!

She's here. She's home!

Her footsteps paint the gravel driveway and the front porch with cookies and vanilla. The chemicals are there as well, but they're faint. I bound up the steps, barking and spinning. I even give my tail a quick chase, which I haven't done since I was a pup. If Esperanza and Nando move any slower, I think I might die. So I try a new tactic.

I race to the door, sit, and then jump and bite the doorknob. Jumping like a rabbit is ridiculous, but I don't care.

My girl is on the other side of this door. So I bounce and nip, bounce and nip, until Nando and Esperanza catch up.

"Easy, girl," Esperanza says, her voice a low whisper. Her hand rests on the knob, teasing me. "She's still tired. She might be sleeping."

Oh, my goodness. I love Esperanza, but now is not the time for all the human words. Sitting back on my haunches, I whimper, trying to hurry her along. And finally—finally—she opens the door. Darting through without looking back, I rocket through the main room, down the short hall, and directly to Cloe's room.

She looks small, lying in bed with the covers pulled up to her chin and her eyes closed. But she looks healthy again, and she smells even better.

Careful not to wake her, I jump quietly onto the bed then crawl on my belly toward her. If nothing else, all the silly games we played on the equipment out back have made me more graceful. By the time Nando and Esperanza reach us, I've snuggled in beside Cloe and nuzzled my head beneath her hand.

Nando and Esperanza curl up in the comfy chair in the corner of the room. My eyelids droop as I melt into the bed. When I open my eyes a little later, the moon shines through the window. Unable to imagine life ever getting any better than this, I lie perfectly still, burrowed in a warm nest beside my girl.

In the morning, I wake to featherlight hands caressing the top of my head. When I open my eyes, I'm nose-to-nose with a smiling Cloe.

"You're a good girl, Stella! Without you, the fire wouldn't have been discovered so fast. You saved the forest from Vern's nephews and their horrible firecrackers," she says, showering the top of my head with kisses. "You saved me, and from what Mom said about the deputy and Vern, I don't think we'll have to worry about those boys causing any problems for a long time."

I smile at her and return each and every kiss.

"Time for breakfast, girls," Esperanza calls from the kitchen, interrupting us.

"Come on, Stella. I smell bacon." Cloe pats her leg and heads for the door.

My toenails clack a merry tune as I prance along the hall behind her. In the kitchen, Cloe sits down to a plate piled with bacon, eggs, and beans. I sit beside her, and it's not because I hope she'll drop food—although that would be amazing—but because I want to be close to her. I want to go where she goes. I want to sleep where she sleeps. I want to play silly games with her and make her laugh. I want to be her best friend.

I may not always be a perfect dog. But I'm *her* dog, and I want her to be *my* girl.

"You look well rested," Esperanza says, sliding into a chair across from us.

Cloe eats with one hand and brushes the top of my head with the other. "I am because I got to sleep with Stella." She shoots pleading, puppy-dog eyes at Esperanza.

My head swivels back and forth between the two of them, wondering what Cloe could be pleading for with that massive plate of food in front of her.

Smiling, Esperanza leans forward and brushes the tip of Cloe's nose with her finger. "You, my sweet girl, are quite the salesperson."

"I don't know what you mean." The hint of a smile tugs at Cloe's lips as she stares at Esperanza with wide eyes.

"You know exactly what I mean. You're trying to convince me to keep Stella as a house dog and a pet."

"Well?"

"Well . . ." She leans back in her chair and crosses her arms. "You don't have to convince me. Stella already did. She's your dog. She loves you. It's obvious. And she's a lot smarter than I've given her credit."

"What do you mean?"

I watch, mesmerized by the piece of bacon Cloe holds near her mouth.

"You remember how funny Stella was acting that day at the hardware store?" She uncrosses her arms and scoots her chair closer to Cloe's.

"Yes."

"Well, she was doing the same exact thing yesterday when we found you in the woods. She was one of the best bomb-sniffing dogs in the business, and apparently, she's using those skills to monitor what's going on physiologically in your body. She knows when you're going to have a seizure, Cloe."

Cloe sets her bacon on the plate, then slides off the edge of the chair and onto the floor. She pulls me into a bear hug. "I knew you were special," she whispers and rubs her face against my neck.

"She's very special. And it doesn't matter what kind of tricks she can perform or what kind of tests she passes, she has a special bond with you. She's your dog, Cloe. And if that means sleeping with a dog in the bed, so be it."

"Did you hear that, girl? You're home," she says as she pulls me into her lap.

I might not understand every word they say, but I like the happy tone of the conversation. And I like the joyful emotions wafting from their skin. So I stand on my back legs, gently rest my front paws on Cloe's chest, and lick her face. She smells and tastes delicious—so delicious I can't stop myself. I *woof*. And they collapse in laughter, right there on the floor.

"I forgot to tell you. You might want to give her a bath. She's going to have important visitors this week."

"Who?" Cloe's grip on me tightens. "They're not going to try to take her from me, are they?"

"Of course not." Esperanza ruffles her hair and stands up. "She's your dog. Come on—let's clean up and take care of the sheep. I'll explain while we work."

I search their faces as they load dishes into the dishwasher, wondering why they sound so serious all of a sudden, but I'm too grateful to be in the house to think about anything else right now.

Right now, I'm going to lie with the cool wood floor against my warm belly. I'm going to savor the smell of bacon painting the kitchen. I'm going to watch my girl and not worry about anything or anyone else for a very long time.

Chapter Twenty-One

The next several days unfold in a hot but comfortable routine. Cloe and I wake together, eat together, play together, and even sleep in the house together. This morning, plump clouds hang low, hugging the mountains surrounding the farm. The unusually crisp air feels delicious on my face and nose.

Yummy smells float from Cloe's treat pouch as we play *watch me* and *touch*. When she gestures toward a series of jumps, I race through the obstacles, eager to please her. After I scramble through the tunnel, she approaches the teetering contraption that makes the loud noises and places a bit of bologna on the end of the board resting on the sand.

I trot over and eat it.

"You're ready, girl," she says and places several more pieces along the upward slant.

Hesitantly, I step from one piece to the next, eating as I go. Before I realize it, I'm well above ground.

"Yes! Yes! Yes!" Cloe inches along beside me, step-by-step.

When I pass the midpoint, the board tips, and I almost freeze.

"Come on, girl. Come on. I've got you," she says, guiding me with a tiny piece of meat along the board as it sinks to the ground with a *thump*. When it hits the ground, she drops to her knees in the sand and opens her arms to me. I leap from the board and into her arms, my tail wagging my entire body.

I can hardly believe what I've done. With Cloe's help, *I did the thing I could not do*. I wish Connie were here to see me. She would be so proud. I pushed past my fear and crossed the unsteady, noisy contraption without freezing. In fact, I've done several things recently that I thought I could not do.

"Come on, girls," Esperanza calls from down the hill, interrupting our celebration. "We've got visitors."

Cloe brushes sand from my chest and kisses me on top of the head. As we head down the hill, I bounce alongside her, enjoying the freedom of being off leash. A small crowd gathers near the barn. Familiar fragrances bombard my nose as we approach—coffee, sandwiches, medicine, fuzzy slippers. But there are less familiar smells as well—humans I don't recognize, all holding small canvas bags.

"She looks great," a man with a deep voice says as we approach.

My ears lift. I glance up at Cloe then squint toward the group of people. My nose twitches, sifting through a symphony of smells.

Cloe gestures toward the man. "It's okay, girl. Go see him."

I trot forward, picking up speed. The yummy scent of one of my favorite humans grows stronger, tickling my nose. My paws kick up gravel. It's Jake! He squats down as I approach. When I leap into his chest, he falls over. The people milling about laugh as I lick his cheek.

"I'm happy to see you too, Stella." He chuckles, his fingers scratching under my chin.

I scramble up his shoulders until he wraps me in his arms. When he stands up, I can see the rest of the people gathered on the grass. My lips pull back in a smile, my tail wagging uncontrollably. Ava's here and Doc Collins. Diana stands behind them with her pizza friend. All the most important people in my life are here—together. My entire body wiggles and squirms, like I've been invaded by a hyperactive squirrel.

"You're a hero, Stella Bella," Esperanza says as she

drapes an arm around Cloe's shoulders. "You're going to be on the news."

Cloe reaches out to rub my head, and I twist toward her. Jake nuzzles the tender spot behind my ear one more time, then he hands me over to her, and I melt against her chest.

"It's not often someone comes along who is a true friend," Cloe says, staring into my eyes. "But I'm so glad you did."

I tilt my head back and howl to show her I remember how much she loved those words when she read them aloud to me that day at the creek.

"Get their picture. That's the one you should use in the newspaper," Ava says.

A man takes out a small machine from his canvas bag. He closes one eye and lifts the contraption to his face. When he clicks a button, a flash of light blinds me. In the momentary blackness, I hear a soothing voice.

"You're a good girl, Stella. You're such a good girl." It's Connie, smiling at me from a cloud of light high above my head. I blink, and she disappears.

When my eyes adjust, I glance around at the humans I love and tell myself that if Connie says I'm a good girl, then I'm a good girl. I could always trust Connie. And I'm learning that I can still trust my nose and myself, too—and Cloe, of course.

Glancing to the sky, I search for Connie one last time, wanting her to know how much she will always mean to me. As I do, the first drops of cool rain fall from the sky and hit my nose. Suddenly, I realize I don't need to prove anything to Connie. I never did. She and I will always be connected, just like Cloe and I will always be connected, just like any good dog and her human will always be connected.

Licking the moisture from my nose and lips, I wag my tail and smile at the friends who love me. As the cool rain washes over us, I close my eyes. My body relaxes against Cloe's warm chest, and I feel safe.

It dawns on me that maybe that's the meaning of true love. Maybe love isn't something that can be earned through good work or destroyed by bad mistakes. Maybe true love is trusting someone or something so much that you feel safe enough to be yourself with them.

Opening my eyes, I turn to Cloe and Esperanza and shower them in kisses—kisses of gratitude, and joy, and something I had to learn to feel again—hope.

Acknowledgments

Stella is possible only because of my supportive pack of friends, family, book lovers, and a lifetime's worth of good dogs.

To my extraordinary agent, Amanda Leuck. Thanks always for believing in me and also for believing in little Stella.

Huge thanks also to the Shadow Mountain team, especially Lisa Mangum and Chris Schoebinger, for loving Stella as much as I do and for making her story come alive.

I'm grateful for teachers and librarians everywhere, who spread the love of reading and improve the lives of so many. Many thanks to these educators and librarians for reading an early draft of *Stella*: Heather Chandler, Millicent Flake, Jennifer Jowett, Sandra Landers, and Amanda Wickman.

ACKNOWLEDGMENTS

Thanks also to Jillian Manning for reading and for the countless suggestions on how to make Stella and her story shine.

Two books were especially important to me in understanding dogs and the way they perceive the world, particularly through their noses: *Being a Dog: Following the Dog into a World of Smell* (Scribner, 2016) and *Inside of a Dog: What Dogs, See, Smell, and Know* (Scribner, 2009), both by Alexandra Horowitz. Thanks for sharing your understanding of dogs with the world.

These people will always be important members of my pack: Emilie Alexander, Amy DeLuca, Holly Bodger, Laura Baker, Mickey Secrist, Nicole Whitmire, Alan Arena, the Dreamweavers, my extended family, my two beautiful children, and all the teachers and students who've made lasting impressions on me and my stories.

And to my husband, Dusty, who takes care of countless responsibilities so that I can pursue all my dreams, including training dogs and writing books.

Discussion Questions

1. Readers can often make predictions about what will happen next in a story when they read. What do you predict life will be like for Stella in the weeks and months after the story ends?
2. Stories have themes or lessons. What do you think is one of the most important lessons that Stella learns in the story? How does this lesson apply to you or your life?
3. Some readers like to make pictures or create movies in their heads while they are reading. What is one scene in the book that really created a movie in your head?
4. *Stella* is interesting because it's told from a dog's point of view. How do you think the story would have been different if it had been told from Cloe's or any other human's point of view?

5. Using details from the story, draw a picture of the farm where Stella and Cloe live and share it with someone. Explain what details you chose to use and why you chose them.

6. Main characters usually grow and change in a story. How did Stella change from the beginning to the end of the story?

7. One of Cloe's favorite books is *Charlotte's Web*. She loves the line where Wilbur says, "It is not often that someone comes along who is a true friend and a good writer." In your own words, explain what it means to be a true friend.

8. All stories have turning points where things go from bad to good or good to bad. What are some of the major turning points in Stella's story?

9. Stella and Nando are both good dogs who truly love their person. How is Stella and Cloe's relationship like Nando and Esperanza's? How are they different?

10. First Lady Eleanor Roosevelt constantly tried to make the world a better place for other people. She delivered speeches and wrote books and is known for many wise sayings, including "You must do the thing you think you cannot do." What do you think the First Lady meant by this advice? How does Stella follow this advice? How could you apply this advice to your own life?

About the Author

Photo provided by the author

MCCALL HOYLE lives in the foothills of the North Georgia Mountains with her husband, children, and an odd assortment of pets. She is a middle school teacher and librarian. When she's not reading, writing, or teaching, she's probably playing with or training one of many dogs. You can learn more about her at mccallhoyle.com.